Death and Duplicity

Death and Duplicity

Lou Korus

Brookins Books LLC
Roseville, Minnesota

Acknowledgments

I would like to thank those who read my first drafts:
Joanne Mellin
Dave and Karen Korus
Theresa Zirwes
Don Hellander
Members of the Sandpoint Chapter of Idaho Writers League
My editor: Kit Cooley of Dream Lizard Creations
Helpful suggestions were provided by:
Mr. Thomas J. Cronin, retired Commander Forensic Services Division, Chicago Police Dept., retired Police Chief Couer d'Alene, ID, and Robert S. West, MD. FACS, retired Coroner in Rural North Idaho

The puzzle in this mystery is for your entertainment. This story is a fictional creation of a family living through devastating circumstances. I hope to live long enough to see major changes in how this country deals with mental illness. May *you* live long enough to decide to make a difference.

– Lou Korus

1

Tom Daniels hadn't seen his son Porter since he had left the dinner table. Daniels put on his sheepskin jacket and heavy boots and went out the front door with his flashlight. He paused in the snow-filled darkness and listened. Nothing but the winter wind. He walked the path to the garage. Seeing no sign of his son, he walked back down the hill. He stopped. The northern Arizona night air was biting cold on his face. Fir trees sighed and he smelled the burning shaggy bark Juniper of his neighbor's fireplace as he trekked up the shoveled path toward his shed. He shivered as he inspected the moonlit expanse of his forested acreage. Daniels took the path over to the shed to the right of the garage located fifty yards north of the house.

"Porter. Porter, is that you? Are you there?" He moved around to the side of the shed when he saw him. Porter was lying on his back, with a .45-caliber gun in close proximity to his open mouth, his winter jacket open, revealing the shirt Tom had given him for Christmas. A pool of blood colored the snow beneath his head. His eyes were wide open, staring upward at nothing.

"This can't be! Porter! Not my son!" Daniels lips parted and he breathed hard, trying to control his emotions. He directed his eyes toward the ground next to his son's body.

"Whose footprints are these?" he stared out into the dark, then brought the flashlight back on the horrifying scene. His mind seemed to stutter.

"Porter, Porter!" his anguished cry filled the cold night air. His body slumped, his shoulders curled. Porter's dog, Lalasa, let out a howl from his pen, a high-pitched eerie sound. Daniels shuddered.

"Shut up you damned devil dog!"

He stood for a long while, trying to comprehend what had happened. His son's dog cried out again, another yowl lasting several seconds.

Daniels heart beat hard, his brows creased and his eyes blurred. His breath curled and hung suspended as he walked about, circling back on his own tracks. He tromped down the snow, obliterating any evidence.

"Goddammit! Whose footprints are these? They're smaller than Porter's feet."

He stomped hard in the snow while sweat gathered in his armpits and his arms flailed about causing the light to ricochet off the tree limbs. His face wrinkled and wrenched with screwed up emotion. He examined the area again and turned his attention back to his son.

"What the hell happened here? You're not supposed to be dead! Wha...?"

Daniels head jerked to the side. Something seemed to move on the other side of the mammoth boulder jutting out a few yards away. "Christina? Jill? Who's there?" *Is that a shadow over there, or hair blowing?*

2

Daniels went back into the house, his face gray with anguish.

His wife, Jill, stood on the staircase, a shawl about her shoulders, her wet slippers leaving tiny puddles on the stairs. She held her body stiff looking like a statue.

Did she follow me out the door? Too damned cold. She would have gone right back in.

He took a towel, bent and wiped her feet. Then he lifted and carried her up the stairs to their bedroom.

"Stay here."

"I heard the dog. What's wrong?" she asked.

"Porter's killed himself."

"Oh dear. Did you feed the dog?" she added.

Daniels moved his eyes over her sweet face.

She's not getting it.

"Don't say a word to anyone, just stay here. Quiet. I'll be back soon," he whispered. He left the bedroom and hastened downstairs and into the den. He sat and stared at the phone.

After several deep breaths, he managed to dial the sheriff's emergency number. Vacillating between extreme stress and forced calm, he thought about the unexplained circumstances.

Son of a bitch! I thought we had this all worked out. Someone's going to pay for this. And I know who!

He waited for the dispatcher to answer. "He's taken his life," he explained. "Out by the shed. No need for sirens. He's gone."

Standing alone in the den, he forced himself to think clearly.

Tell them only the facts. Keep things simple. The sheriff and the EMTs don't know anything and they won't know much when they leave. He sighed heavily.

He reassured himself over and over the nightmare would go away, allowing a sense of calm to revisit his mind. Daniels closed the door to the den, pulled his sheepskin jacket back on and stepped out onto the covered cement patio. He waited by the front door until Sheriff Brown's car pulled up. The passenger door opened and Marianne Lawler stepped out.

Daniels eyes opened wide. *For the love of almighty, he lets her ride along for this? That nosy woman has to know everything that's going on.* He shook his head in disbelief as the sheriff walked toward him.

"Daniels. I'm sorry to be here under these circumstances. Do you want to walk with me to where you found him? The medical examiner will be here any minute now and we'll make this as easy as possible for you." The sheriff pressed forward closer to Daniels. Daniels's head swung around and he glared in Marianne's direction. "She's not coming," he said.

"No, no. She's a friend, and with me because, well, that's not important right now," Brown explained. "She'll wait in the car."

Daniels saw the glare the sheriff threw in Marianne's direction and watched as she got back into the vehicle.

Sheriff Brown took Daniel's arm and urged him to direct him toward the location of the body. The medical examiner arrived and the ambulance with the paramedics joined them. An uneasy quiet engulfed the snowy landscape until they began their questions. Small puffs of moistened air punctuated each sentence.

Daniels's body began to relax under the calming influence of the sheriff's firm grasp.

The Medical Examiner began his questioning.

"Suicide? You're sure this is your son?"

"Yes. His shirt. I gave it to him."

"Anyone else hear anything? Neighbors?"

"They're all too far away."

"Take notice of anything unusual?"

"No."

"Who else lives here?" he continued.

"My wife and myself."

"Where is she?"

"She's not well. In bed. Asleep."

"Where is the gun? Did you remove it?"

Daniels eyes widened. "I don't know. No."

"Review your movements with me after you discovered your son's body."

"I went in the house, put my wife to bed, called 911, and waited out front for the ambulance to get here."

"You didn't return to your son's location."

"No."

"You didn't see or hear anyone else on the property that evening before his death, or after?"

"No."

"Someone took the gun. Do you have any idea who would do that? Your wife, possibly?"

"She is … her memory … is … somewhat compromised. She is not yet fully aware of our boy's death."

"I see."

The Medical Examiner took the sheriff a few steps away from Daniels and expressed his concerns to him.

"Sheriff Brown, it is obvious by the way the right arm and hand and the position of the finger and the exit wound that this young man killed himself. I am puzzled why or who would remove the weapon. Did he describe the gun? Then we'd know he saw it."

"No. We haven't discussed any of the circumstances since I got here. Most unusual, I agree. Doesn't seem like Daniels was even aware that the gun was taken. It's all in the report and I'll follow up on this, for sure."

"Ballistics will confirm the type of weapon used, but we'll have to hope the gun turns up somewhere on this property. With more snow coming, well, I don't know. See if you can find out if they may have been expecting any visitors, or if he's noticed any unwanted guests, possibly hunters up here without his permission."

Daniels thought their consultation would never end. He felt he could fall apart any second. He searched the sheriff's face for reassurance. Sheriff Brown turned back toward him and nodded his head as if to encourage him.

Brown returned to Daniels's side. "The medical examiner will want to know how you wish to take care of your son's body."

Daniel sighed deeply, looked down at the ground. "He'll be cremated. Burial of his ashes will be in Tucson; his home is there." He glared at both men hoping they would take their leave, knowing that wouldn't happen.

Just get the hell out of here and leave us alone. I've got some serious thinking to do.

After what seemed hours passed, the medical examiner and the ambulance left with Porter's body.

Staring at the imprint in the snow where his son had died, he felt the cold of the wind penetrate and sting his cheeks. Soon his neck and back became stiff and he opened his mouth as if to speak. Slowly he came back to reality.

Sheriff Brown and Daniels walked to the front porch together. Brown put his hand on Daniels' upper arm and squeezed it, searching his eyes.

"I am so sorry for your loss."

Daniels stared back at the sheriff for a long moment then dropped his gaze to his boots where it remained until the sheriff got into his car and pulled away. He breathed heavily in and out, his arms folded tightly against his chest, rocking slightly as he observed the taillights fading into the night. Alone at last, his heavy sobs came out in a torrent of clouds as his angry words filled the night.

"Some people never get things right. Ever!"

* * *

DANIELS WENT TO HIS bedroom and undressed quietly so he would not wake his sleeping wife. He felt cold and unsettled. Lying in the dark, his lids closed tightly and sleep came with dreams that were full of frightening images. He tossed and turned.

The next morning he rose early and walked to the bedroom window. His fingers went to his face, his nails resting tight on his lips as if he could hold back the foul words in his thoughts from tumbling out.

Glancing over at Jill, peaceful in her slumber, he dressed, being careful not to disturb her. He went downstairs and picked up his coat off of the couch, walked outside to the kennel and brought his dog, Rogue, into the snowy yard, leaving Porter's dog, Lalasa alone, sulking beside the spot where his master had died.

"Well, Rogue, some son-of-a-bitch has killed him. I know that for sure. Porter had no reason to do this to himself. We, I, had it all planned. That's right. Planned. Now we need answers, that's what we need, Rogue. Answers. You and me. We'll hunt him down. Find the gun he used. You can help with that schnoz of yours. Smell him out. You can do that for me. I've got something you can get a scent from. Where the hell did I put it? I'd like to strangle him with my own hands. Now, how do you suppose I'm going to find him again? That damned brother-in-law of mine! How did he screw this up? Huh?" The dog sat by his boot, looking up into his eyes with his head tilted as if waiting for further instruction.

Sensing his master's anxiety, Rogue trembled. Daniels cast a glance toward the place where he had discovered his son's body.

"This is unbelievable! It should have been different," he said to Rogue.

No new snow had fallen. The cold morning air stung him through his open jacket. His footsteps quickened as he neared the site. Seeing the snow shovel propped up against the shed, he hurried to pick it up. He shoveled furiously and soon the imprints left by the body and all the footprints were gone. The sight of the dark splotches of blood made him shake. Rogue got up and started in his direction. Daniels commanded him to sit and stay.

"You're not going to get a sniff of this. No way! You stay," he shouted when Rogue attempted to get up again.

He dug deep into a nearby pile of snow and pounded it on top of the areas he wanted to obliterate. Anger spilled out of his mouth with obscenities. He stood still, catching his breath when he finished the job. *What in the hell happened to the gun?*

He put the shovel inside the door of the shed and went up the stairs into the secluded office with Rogue at his heels. The dog padded over to the bed next to the heater and laid himself down on it with an audible groan. Daniels slumped at his desk, holding his head in his hands. A moment later his attention went to his computer monitor. He began typing words, changing the text many times. He rose, kicked the wastepaper basket beside the desk, watching the crumpled up discarded email attempts he'd made scatter across the floor while Rogue sat up visibly startled. Daniels decided to try once more to compose an explanation for neighbors and friends. The note was short and contained little information about Porter and what happened the previous night. He couldn't risk allowing them to draw any conclusions from his message on their own.

"I hope they don't read too much into it. Wonder if anyone will guess the truth? *And why would they? I* don't even know the truth! Our plan got all messed up! Who else was out there in the woods last night? Whose footprints did I cover up? Jill's feet were wet. Was she there?" Rogue sighed, lowered himself back into his bed, and rested his head on his paws.

Daniels sat at his desk several more minutes. "We went over and over it. Simple. It was simple! Nothing should have gone wrong. You hear that, Rogue? Nothing." Daniels eyes followed Rogue as his dog got up from its bed and came to his side.

Daniels got up from his chair, stared at the floor, and then made his way slowly down the steps. He took his dog back to the kennel, giving him a pat on the back, and returned to the house.

He went up the stairs to wake Jill and encouraged her to dress and come down to the kitchen.

"Yes. I'm coming. Help me with this, please," she asked holding her garment up to him. He buttoned the shirt she chose and slipped her shoes onto her feet.

"Comb your hair a little, okay?"

"I can do that," she told him, smiling back.

Jill washed her face, peered into the mirror, tilted her head to one side and then the other and smoothed her hair with her hand. She went downstairs to the spacious kitchen. At her urging, the kitchen design had become similar to the one in her parents' home in Phoenix. Daniels smiled as he watched her, knowing she found comfort in the familiarity of it. He noticed her staring at the open refrigerator door.

"How about some butter to go with those muffins?" Daniels suggested.

"Of course. Good idea." She reached in and took the covered dish out and placed it onto the counter.

"I've got the coffee going."

"It smells so good. Can I drink some now?"

An hour later Daniels answered the urgent sound of the doorbell. He wondered who would be there.

"Well, hello neighbors!" he said, as he swung the door open wide, the smell of freshly brewed coffee wafting into the front hallway. "Sunshine and good friends greet me this fine day. Do come in."

The couples who came to see the Daniels were friends as well as neighbors. He noted their expressions reflected sympathy as their brows were slightly raised and their eyes large and open as if to question him.

"We received your email, Tom. Tragic. We wanted to tell you both how sorry we are," Jack Hanson began.

"Yes." Daniels paused. "Yes, of course."

"You must be devastated over the loss of your son," Mary Dwyer said. "I am so so sorry." Her husband Fred nodded in agreement.

Daniels observed how his friend's faces revealed strange looks he didn't understand. Daniels pasted a pleasant look on his face to hide his thoughts. *Are they hiding something? They may think I'm in shock over my son's death, or I'm relieved this schizophrenic nightmare is over. The boy was mad, sometimes. I couldn't handle it. But what else might they wonder.*

The Dwyers and Hansons joined Jill in the kitchen. She wore jeans and a red plaid shirt, and greeted them warmly. "How nice to find visitors in my kitchen." She poured the coffee and offered muffins, her sweet smile reflecting no hint of the previous night's deadly out-come.

Conversation became awkward as minutes passed and when the coffee and muffin supply dwindled, the guests began to exit into the front hallway.

"Let us know if there is anything we can do," Hanson's wife's words as they put on their coats.

Daniels closed the door behind them with a sigh of relief.

* * *

THE SNOW CRUNCHED underfoot as they made their way toward the road.

"Jill's memory seems to be getting worse. I'm sure she didn't realize why we came," Jean Hanson commented. "Did you notice how happy she was to see us?"

"She's lost her flare for fashionable clothes, too. Her outfit resembled clothing you'd expect to see in a man's closet," Mary Dwyer said.

"I think there's a medical issue with Jill, don't you?" Jack Hanson asked.

"And Tom seemed pretty upbeat. Strange," Fred Dwyer added.

"I'm puzzled," Jack said. "I wouldn't want to be in their situation. Unimaginable."

"I thought Tom looked terrible. Bags under his eyes and all," Jean Hanson said.

"Did he say anything about what happened?" Fred asked.

"Not a word. He's going to need to talk to somebody, wouldn't you think?" Jack answered.

"For sure," they answered in unison.

They walked silently up the rest of the driveway with only murmured goodbyes as they took separate paths to their own homes.

* * *

LATER THAT DAY, Daniels sat alone again in his office. He glanced at the beige wall, looking at the photo Jill had hung above his desk. It was of Jill and her brother John with their parents, the Andersons. He smiled to himself, remembering how Porter and Christina referred to them as Granna and Granpa because of the difficulty they both had pronouncing ds. The family in the photo stood on the front porch of their home in Phoenix, Arizona dressed formally as if ready to go somewhere. *Probably a fundraiser of some sort.* He shifted in his chair, remembering how Jill's parents had given him a chilly reception when they first met. His hands dampened as he remembered it. He smiled to himself recalling the exhilaration he'd felt when her family eventually warmed to his jokes and exaggerated accomplishments. His determination to win them over worked. *Some of their well-to-do friends became customers, buying up my best hand carved sculptures. They weren't the only ones with some class.*

Daniels studied John Anderson's young face in the photo. An uncomfortable conversation had taken place with Jill's brother before Daniels and Jill married. *Even then he had a way about him before he became a psychiatrist. He had the ability to get you to confide in him about things you hadn't planned to say out loud.*

"You've never spoken much about your father," John had said. "What did he do for a living?"

"A salesman." Daniels answered.

"You took after him, then."

"I am *nothing* like my father, and don't you forget that! I hated the man!"

"That's a very strong indictment, Tom. I've noticed how angry you become whenever the subject of your parents comes up. This kind of issue is best dealt with and I'd be happy to recommend someone for you to talk to."

"Leave it alone, John! It's none of your business. I don't want you to make any mention of this, ever again!"

Daniels face reddened with the memory of the exchange.

It's today I'm concerned about. And last night. For god's sake, John is a leader in his field of psychiatry and he was so positive Porter's latest sessions showed real progress.

His thoughts went back to John's handling of Porter's mental problems. He'd been under his care for several years being treated and counseled for schizophrenia. A year of continuous bullying by a former high school acquaintance by the name of Carson Dittle nearly pushed Porter to his breaking point. Anderson had found it difficult to keep his patient on track, but with diligence, he had made some progress with Porter. His nephew was taking his medicines faithfully and keeping his appointments, so he agreed to let him come home for a visit before he and Daniels went ahead with their plan.

Daniels interrupted his thoughts, and opened the file cabinet. He poured himself a drink and began talking out loud to himself.

"How many times when he was little did I look in on the boy, lying on the floor with his mother right beside him, patiently waiting for him to end one of his frequent tantrums? Drove me nuts. I let Jill handle him for the most part. Porter was annoying and demanding. I loved him, but I couldn't be with him when he was like that. Jill goes through life with no prejudices. She learned that from her mother. She treats everyone with gracious tolerance. Porter seemed to get through high school okay.

When he was in college is when he fell apart. That was it for me. I washed my hands of him. Be damned if I was going to pay for fines and damages and unpaid bills! Couldn't stand the drama. Jill hung in there getting him out of scrapes and got him to stick with John's therapy. He actually got better after that. And now this! Dammit!

Porter was feeling so much better. He told John he was looking forward to spending some time with us up here in Spartan. And he said Carson Dittle hadn't been seen in his neighborhood for some time. No phone calls from him, no letters in the mail, and he hadn't figured out his new email address. His life had been made a lot easier. He even started sleeping more than two hours at a time. His face showed some color when he spoke, according to John. And no voices telling him to do god-knows-what! At the end of their session John told me he had let Porter in on our plan. What details did John mess up? It certainly wasn't me. He hardly had anything he needed to do. I was the one... "

Daniels's eyes refocused and he stopped his one sided conversation.

"I'm sick of talking to myself. There's no one. I can't discuss this with anyone!" He became agitated, flexing his shoulders up and down, lifting a foot and putting his heel down hard. His face flushed. He was frustrated with Porter's death and his deduction that someone must have gotten wind of their plans and turned the tables on them. The drink in his hand slopped over the edge of the glass when he slammed it down against the desk.

3

Carson Dittle kept busy the day Porter visited with his psychiatrist. He peered through his fingerprinted glasses at his computer screen as he navigated around various websites.

Carson Dittle was twenty-one years old, had deep-set blue eyes and was of average height. His forehead protruded and was accented by almost feminine-looking arched brows that expressed profound arrogance. His dark hair fell over his forehead in an Elvis sort of way.

"That son-of-a-bitch's gotta be somewhere online," he said, spraying little spots of spittle on the computer screen. He pulled his tee shirt forward far enough to smear the spots, clouding his view even more.

"To hell with him. I'll find him later. His blue eyes narrowed. He opened Facebook pages where images of women filled his screen.

"Hello, stupid girl. Still going on about the asshole you're dating? Little does she know what I have in mind." His upper lip rose up over his eyetooth giving him a wolf-like appearance. He focused in on his prey, taking pleasure in typing idle conversation intent on doing something evil.

"They think I can't find them. But I know exactly where all of them hang out. Even Porter Daniels. That jerk will be twitching again with fear any day now. I let him think I was gone. Ha! Gone further with my plan, that's what."

Carson's fingers flew across the keyboard as he accessed every bit of information he could possibly retrieve. The machine hummed into action as it printed out what he wanted. The three-ring binder got thicker as he added paper after paper containing the personal information he studied each night before retiring.

He put the binder back into the locked metal box in his closet.

Carson Dittle rubbed his hand back and forth over the back of his neck. A half-smile slithered across his lips as he remembered the last time he had taunted Porter.

* * *

"I watched you coming out of the library, Porter. You look sick."

"Thanks."

"No, stupid. Really sick."

"You've got a right to your opinion. Leave me alone, Dittle."

Dittle stepped behind Porter, following him for several blocks.

"I heard Joanie say your breath is bad, dude."

"So?"

"And Mary said your brain is so fried, you stutter."

"Shut up."

"I read your e-mail to Joanie. You must be desperate,

dude. She'll do anybody. Pleading with her to forgive you. Couldn't give it to her, huh?"

Carson Dittle laughed. He sounded almost hysterical.

Porter began to sweat. As they neared City Park he was afraid he wouldn't be able to outrun Dittle. He could feel his breath on the back of his neck.

Dittle closed in when they reached the park and shoved Porter, whose knees buckled and he fell to the ground with a grunt.

"Look at daddy's little boy. Oh, you are so sweet. I'm going to kick all that sweet out of you." This time he didn't smell the acrid aroma of fear coming from his victim. He'd have to do more, push up the hurt.

Dittle kicked Porter hard in the belly and once on the side of his head. His heavy boot knocked the wind from him. Kicking at his ribs, he gauged carefully how hard he swung his leg.

"Don't want to break them, little boy, do I. Just want to give you a little tingle. Saving it for another time."

Dittle watched as Porter closed his eyes tight and brought himself into a fetal position.

"Get up, you fool. Or are you not man enough to take me on? Come on!" Dittle's mood darkened and a deep guttural laugh slipped from his half-closed mouth. His thoughts turned to the times he saw his mother fly up off the couch to retaliate against his physically abusive father. His father would meet her with a hard backhand and she'd land sprawled on the floor, whimpering. A red welt almost always rose on her cheek after that. It made him feel good that she got what he thought she deserved.

Porter coughed, calculated a measured pause while he gathered his strength. He didn't move until he was ready. He rolled onto his other side and stood up faster than Dittle could react. Porter grabbed Dittle around his neck and threw him to the hard dirt.

Laughing again, Dittle took his time getting back on his feet. "That was lame, dude." He came at Porter with enough fury to put him down and helpless in an instant. Porter thought the pummeling wasn't going to stop. The throbbing in his back, sides, and belly made him feel nauseous.

Finally, Dittle brushed his hands together, glaring down at his victim. There was a hint of the smell of bile that brought a half-smile to his face.

"I'll get you worse next time, you creepy crawler." He kicked the dirt into Porter's face.

"Want 'cha to know I've cooked up some fun for you. You'll love it. There's not a damned thing you can do about it, either."

Dittle sauntered off and turned the corner of the park where he walked among the trees that would keep him out of Porter's view.

He stayed out of sight, watching.

Porter lay still for several minutes. Finally, he sat up and looked around the park.

Dittle, watching, could almost hear Porter groan with pain when he struggled to his feet and headed toward home, holding his stomach. He'd held his gait in check, unaware of Dittle following him, using his binoculars to watch and enjoy every moment of his victim's obvious pain. Each barely discernible limp brought satisfaction to Dittle's excited mind. He could see Porter's efforts to get up the apartment stairs was huge. He watched until, with great effort and labored breathing, Porter disappeared up the stairs to his apartment and closed the door.

Coming back to the present, Dittle walked to the window and stared out for a moment. He wiped his brow with his hand, smearing the sweat onto the outside of his pants. *He's so easy. I can pick and choose when to find him. Ah, but that was last week. I have more to do.*

He closed the room's blackout drapes. He smirked as he reviewed his appointment with his psychiatrist Dr. Anderson earlier in the day.

Anderson has no idea how many papers I stole from his files and copied, especially the ones about Porter! Anderson thinks I'm making progress. And I am! I have found out even more ways to torture Porter.

He showered and shaved, applied a generous amount of musk-smelling aftershave to his cheeks and neck. He removed his glasses and replaced them with contact lenses. He glanced in the mirror with cocky approval. Dittle chose his clothing carefully, opting for jeans and a polo shirt to blend in with every other college student in the neighborhood.

He opened the small carved box on top of the chest of drawers. He fingered something, then picked it up and rolled it around in his hand, moving his jaw first to the left and then to the right. Heaving a long drawn out sigh, he put the object back in the box.

His father had dropped his tie clasp one evening as he dressed to go out. "Boy, come and find my clasp." As Dittle scrambled around the floor desperate to retrieve it to gain his father's approval, his mother came in the room. He heard the hate and imagined the fury in her eyes as she shrieked at his father. "Going out again? With one of them?"

So many words and accusations. He covered his ears to keep out the remembered sounds. "Whyn't you just go and never come back!"

He was only fifteen, and it would be the last time he would see his father. He had cowered in the darkness of the bedroom until he was sure his Mother would not return to the room. He'd held onto the tie clasp as if he could will his father to come back to get it. He slept on the floor that night until a loud thud woke him. He crept out into the living room and found his mother there, on the couch, dead, and already cold to the touch. The stink of booze drifted up into his nostrils. He picked up the empty liquor bottle from the floor. The half-empty glass was on the magazine table next to the couch. He sniffed it and then downed the rest of it with a shudder and then tossed the bottle into the trash container. He left the front door open as he walked out to begin his life on the streets.

Dittle's hand rested on the top of the box for several more seconds. He turned abruptly, left the box and his past memories to go out into the night to flush out his prey.

Christina. I almost forgot. Porter's sister wanted to meet me. I can have my way with both of them.

He glided smoothly down the stairs making little noise. Outside, he glanced up at his window, reassuring himself that no one could see the light radiating out from his private sanctuary. The anticipation of what the evening promised showed in his walk, a swagger of sensual hip movements, practiced to seduce. He'd seen his father leave their home in the same manner many times. He'd practiced until it was easy for him to copy the walk, the attitude.

He walked past the park, smiling at the thought of his attack on Porter. Several blocks further, he boarded a bus. It rambled slowly along the street, stopping at the designated pick-up points. Dittle watched the buildings and people pass by the window, his thoughts on the evening ahead. A dark-haired woman, dressed scantily in a short skirt and tight tube top, wearing high heels, smiled and waved at the passing bus. His heart stopped. He drew in a long breath and swallowed hard trying to hold down the horror making his stomach churn.

It can't be her! She was cold. Dead. I touched her. I know what death looks like. He rubbed his thighs over and over in an attempt to calm himself.

4

Christina Daniels, aged nineteen and two years younger than her brother Porter, was visiting her Uncle John and his wife Anne for a few days. As the favorite and only niece, they loved her unannounced visits. She exuded a spark of intelligence and humor as well as an inner beauty and outward confidence. Anne wondered why John's parents became Christina's mentors when she'd turned sixteen and how it had influenced her life. Questions to John about Christina's circumstances remained unanswered. Apparently he knew nothing of her private life.

Between John's patient appointments, Christina had been in the hallway on her way to the kitchen when she overheard her uncle talking to her father on the telephone. The conversation was one sided, but she had caught enough to get the idea of what her father and uncle were planning. A quick look through his office file cabinet and later, as she opened his computer files, she had more than enough information to confirm her suspicions. She would have to act quickly to stop it. She knew she could accomplish what was necessary without them being a part of it.

Upon her return to her apartment in Tucson where she stayed while on assignment, she placed a call to Carson Dittle and asked to meet him.

She dressed with care that evening. He had never tried anything physical with her in public, but to be safe, meeting Dittle at a busy bar would provide the protection she felt necessary. She chose a dark colored pant and a jean jacket with a plain white shirt to wear. As she picked up her perfume bottle she raised her eyebrows and set it back down. She thought an enticing aroma of anything should be the last thing she'd want tonight.

She had not forgotten the incident in her bedroom when she was a freshman in high school.

She had finished her homework in her room and went to the bureau to take out her pajamas. She entered the bathroom she shared with her brother, turning on the water in the tub. After testing the temperature and pulling the handle to enable the shower, she had undressed and got in. The warm spray of the water lulled her into a peaceful calm after the stress of studying for tomorrow's algebra test. Stepping out of the bathtub, she carefully patted her silken hair to damp dry and then her body. She slipped into her pajamas and dashed into her bed and fell into a light slumber. As she was turning over onto her right side some moments later, something moved near the doorway.

As her bedroom door opened a crack, the hall light gave just enough illumination to allow her some sight. Opening her eyes to a slit, she sucked in her breath slowly. Someone was in her room, looking down at her. Exhaling silently, she watched the shadow, trying to discern who was there. *Focus. Don't swallow. So hard not to make noise.*

After a few silent breaths she realized it was not Porter. *Breathe slowly. Don't give yourself away!* The shadowy figure moved closer to her bed. *God! I'm not going to panic.* As the figure stopped again, Christina opened her eyes as wide as she dared.

Oh! It's that pervert Dittle! I thought he went home right after I came in to study. Breathe.

She turned over giving out a small, sleepy sigh and settled down into pretend sleep. With her eyes still squinting, she saw the reflection on the wall she faced. The shadow began to recede. Again, the door opened enough to let in a slit of light from the hallway. It closed without a sound.

Her heart still beat hard as she worked to conquer her fright. *How long had he been watching me? In the shower? No. I would have seen him when I got out.*

She coaxed her breathing to return to normal, and remembered what Granna Anderson's people had told her. "Keep your cool and always have the advantage."

He doesn't know I saw him. That's my advantage. I'll get that depraved creep in more trouble than he can handle. She could not understand why Porter ever asked Dittle over after school. *Was he trying to be friendly so that jackass would stop hounding him?*

* * *

CHRISTINA'S NECK HAIRS raised as she relived the anxiety she'd felt the moment she realized she wasn't alone. *I promised myself I'd learn everything I needed to know so I would never feel helpless again.*

She arrived at the agreed destination and entered by

the back door, hoping to spot Dittle before he noticed her. The loud music and the fast-talking unpredictable conversations of the patrons filled the room. The smell of beer and booze nicked at her senses. She scanned the room and found an empty booth near the exit and got a visual of Dittle's location. She slid in the seat and motioned to the waitress.

"I want charged water. Would you get a beer for the dark-haired fellow, the one with his hand on the butt of the redhead over there?"

"Why sure. I'll be back with your drink in a sec. Do you want a slice of lime with that?"

Christina smiled and nodded yes.

The server brought the beer to Dittle. He leaned toward her, and she pointed in Christina's direction. He picked up the stein and strolled over to the booth, positioning himself close to her.

"Are you going to sit down or stand there and stare at me?"

Dittle didn't take his eyes off Christina as the waitress delivered her drink to the table. "I'm taking in all of you, Christina. The long blond hair, the breasts trying to bust out of that oh-so-tight jacket. Give me a peek. Come on!"

Christina gave him a half smile and resisted the temptation to roll her eyes. "You'll never change, you pervert. Listen up. Get over your ogling. Sit."

Dittle sat, leaned forward, and continued staring at her chest. "I'm listening."

"I want your attention, right here, right into my eyes. Got it? I'm only going through this once." She paused for emphasis. "I need your help with a family problem."

"This oughta be good. Spit it out."

"Obviously you... enjoy, harassing my brother. How would you like to help me get rid of him?"

"I'm intrigued."

"Porter's antics are getting worse and he's causing me trouble. I've had enough. My folks are, never mind. He's a wretched little whiner and his crap is going to stop." Christina recalled the anguished look in her mother's eyes whenever she'd returned from one of her trips to get Porter out of trouble and her father's anger and indifference.

Dittle rubbed his hands together showing his excitement.

"Now I'm hot and bothered. Women like you with ideas like that turn me on."

"I'll meet you again tomorrow night at 7:00 P.M. Different place. You know the bar called Rodeo City? No drinking, either. You need to be clear headed to understand what I am planning. When the time comes, if you follow my directions, I am going to let you do something you are going to love."

Dittle stood, moved out of the booth and put his hands flat on the table. He leaned in and sniffed at her hair. "Mmmm. I'll be there. Count on it."

Christina shuddered. She turned to get a glimpse of him as he returned to the bar. He didn't lose any time reacquainting himself with the redhead and placing his hand back on its original location.

Convinced Dittle was engrossed with the girl, she took the opportunity to slide out of the booth, making her way to the exit and into the warmth of the evening.

Christina had experience of her own with Dittle's harassment tactics. Somehow he'd found her email and had sent suggestive messages at first. When the phone calls followed, she laughed and played along with him instead of showing any fear, which she was sure he wanted. It became a standoff. He'd keep trying to upset her and she managed to diffuse the conversations.

She was sure she could convince him to follow her lead and would finally put an end to his messing with her, if she could keep his attention on Porter. Getting Porter out of the way was her prime concern.

* * *

THE SCHEDULED MEETING with Dittle at Rodeo City went exactly as Christina had planned.

"This is what I want you to do, Dittle. You've had your fun with Porter, now you're going to have the opportunity to finish him off in grand style."

"Do you know that your tits are blooming right out of your tee shirt?"

"Shut your mouth. This is serious business. You want in, you're going to have to lose that kind of filth. Understand?"

Dittle chose not to answer. He just stared at her.

"Porter is going to be at Mom and Dad's place. I'll get you the fare to fly to Phoenix. The bus will take you the rest of the way. Then I'll come to get you. Meet me in the back alley by The Hitching Post. Bring a gun."

"I'm gonna off him?"

"What do you think?"

"Do I get to terrorize him first?"

"Whatever works."

Dittle's eyes were bright with anticipation. His breath

came in short gasps.

"No drugs, Carson. Got it?"

"If you say so."

"I say so."

Christina hoped he would comply. She needed him to be quick and accurate.

***

Dittle rose early the next day. He opened the box on his dresser, pushed aside the tie clasp and pulled out a small baggy of weed. He took out what he wanted and lit the illegal joint. The long inhale gave him the calm he desired. Desperate for ideas he tried to imagine how he would push his most prized victim to the edge of death. His mind played out several scenes. *I can push him around, hurt him a little, bring up all the nasty stuff I know about him. I know. I'll pin him down and whisper all that in his ear, all the time twisting his arm exacting the pain he needs to feel. Maybe I'll shoot him in the ear after that. The noise in his head! It will be rad! But I don't know what she's got in mind.*

Dittle dialed Christina's number.

"Look. I need more information. How's this gonna work?"

"Not on the phone. Don't call me again. Meet me at the mall in an hour."

Christina found an empty bench and waited. Dozens of shoppers passed her by with Dittle not in sight. He finally showed a half-hour late.

"You're late! Look at you. Your pupils are dilated and the whites are red."

"You look, well, babe. Sexy. Want me?"

"Get real. And don't breathe on me." Christina edged away from him. "Why are you late?"

"Traffic."

"I don't think so. I know where you live. It doesn't take that long to get here."

Dittle's eyes opened wide. He shifted back and forth on his feet sifting the knowledge through his head that she knew his address.

"Get a grip, you dope. Think you are the only person in the world able to track someone unnoticed?"

Dittle opened his mouth to speak as a drop of moisture escaped from the side.

"Wha... What else do you know, bitch?"

"Makes you nervous, huh? Get over it and listen."

They stared at each other waiting for one or the other to give in.

After a moment, Dittle dropped his eyes to his feet. "So what's this plan of yours?"

"I'm giving you an opportunity. You already know what it is. You don't need to know any more than that. Scare the crap out of him and let him take care of himself."

"I don't get to do it?"

"No, stupid. Lead him to it."

"When?"

"Next week. You'll hear from me."

"Huh. Should be fun to watch."

"Whatever. Get out of here. I don't want to be seen with you."

"But, babe!"

"Git!" Christina's face scrunched in disgust as she

watched him leave. She got up and walked quickly in the opposite direction. She ducked into a small store and pretended to be looking over the merchandise with her eyes glued on the front window making sure he had not doubled back to follow her.

A small porcelain doll caught her attention. It was sitting on a satin blanket with its hand resting on a lace pillow, dressed in a white on white embroidered smock. There was a dainty pearl bracelet draped across its fingers. She smiled to herself. It resembled the one Granpa Anderson had given her on her eighth birthday. She had opened the door to the library, and run in looking for her Granpa. She recognized some of the men and women who were frequent dinner guests. Others were new to her and they appeared to be important people. The men were dressed in suits and ties and the ladies garments were tailored and subtle in color. All eyes in the room fastened on her. She couldn't tell if they were alarmed or annoyed. Granna came to her side, took her hand and guided her out the door.

"Mustn't interrupt Granna's private meetings, my dear. Granpa will come to find you when he's finished. We have a lovely surprise for you. Go up to your room now. Be a good girl." Granna leaned over and gave her a kiss on the cheek and squeezed her hand and smoothed the hair she'd made into French braids so often. "All this is for you; you'll see when you're a big girl. Run along, now."

Porter had found the pearl bracelet their grandparents had given her on her dresser one day. He took it and dangled it in front of her, taunting her and making gestures as if he would throw it out the window unless she promised to let him play the part of the king in their next play. Her answer of "maybe" was not good enough. He yanked on the bracelet, breaking it, and laughed as the little pearls rolled around on the wood floor. She had held her tears until after he left the room, while he giggled at his ability to make her mad.

She left the store and her memories when she felt sure she had not been followed.

5

As Christina Daniels made her plans, Tom Daniels reflected on his own course of action. He called his brother-in-law and they discussed their present situation.

"You figure out a way to get him here?" Daniels asked.

"Under control," John's reply.

"How will I know?"

"The date is set; I've already given you that. I'll send a signal on your cell phone. Make sure you leave it on."

"Alright. How are you going to...?"

"No more discussion on the phone, Tom. Just do as we planned."

"Got it. Is Christina still with you?"

"No. Don't know where she is right now."

"Make sure she doesn't know anything."

"Of course. No more contact until it's over, you understand?"

"Yes." Daniels hung up the phone and remained in his chair at his desk. He thought about Christina.

He was surprised when she had asked to come home after she'd been gone for two years. When she asked to help in his business, he wondered how she had acquired her computer skills.

"I've watched you and have seen the results of the work you are doing for me. Where did you go to school?" Daniels asked.

"California schools were good, Dad."

"Thinking of college?"

"Not really. I've had some very good jobs and I'd like to continue in that field."

"Which is?"

"Dad, we have a lot of orders to fill here and the warehouse is down on inventory."

"Heard from your Granna Anderson lately? I thought I overheard you talking to her the other day on the phone."

Christina met his eyes with a blank look and no response. She returned her attention to the monitor and began talking on her phone's headset.

Christina worked hard to help her father. A year passed and she explained she wanted to return to living on her own. Her parents reluctantly agreed. She would go back to a life that they would not be privy to.

Daniels felt bewildered when Christina remained distant and uncommunicative.

As the days went by without Christina's presence and Porter away at college, melancholy wrapped itself around Jill like a lightweight shawl that never gave enough warmth or comfort.

"I miss her, Tom. She's so bright and innovative. What does she do? Where does she go?"

"I really couldn't tell you, Jill." He recognized a glimmer of the sharp intellect she had once possessed.

"Porter's in trouble again, Tom. I need to go to Tucson again."

"Take care of it. I hate watching you run to his side

every time he causes problems."

"I know you can't face it, Tom, but he needs somebody's help and since you aren't willing to help, I'll do everything I can."

"When will you leave?"

"Leave? Oh. Soon."

Daniels watched her eyes lose their focus and he knew she was no longer thinking in the present.

On Jill's best days she spent time in their home, wandering about admiring her handpicked decorations. Those things evoked comfort, calm, and pleasant memories, especially the vases and paintings given to them by her parents. She enjoyed the long, cold nights in front of the fireplace and sunny days. The growing number of silences that filled their home didn't enter her consciousness.

6

Jill Daniels' childhood home, in Phoenix Arizona, was situated on an acre of land near the mountains. It rose three stories high with expansive windows overlooking the circular drive paved with brick and lined with palm trees. The spacious front porch boasted several large cement columns supporting the upper floors. Trellises on either side allowed the bougainvillea vines to climb up and provide brilliant color and privacy. There were many orange and lemon trees on the back of the property. The heady scent emitted from the small citrus orchard heralded the onset of spring each year.

Early in their marriage, Tom and Jill visited her parents.

"Look John! Isn't it just wonderful?"

"Too big and it's too damned hot here."

The Andersons were a prominent family with extensive ties within the philanthropic community. Her parents afforded Jill and her brother freedoms not many teenagers were allowed. They attended fundraising galas that often went late into the evenings. The Anderson's felt social graces were as important as excelling in schools and would help their children to connect with people who could open doors to good career choices.

The interiors of homes visited on those occasions were of interest to Jill. As a youngster she sought out the rooms closed off from visitors to observe the decor, forming ideas of her own that she would use later in her life. The Southwestern art and colors were her particular favorites. She was amazed by the cool afforded by the thick adobe walls in one home constructed in the early 1930's that needed no modern day air conditioning. The residence boasted a collection of both American Indian and American cowboy art. She studied the bronze sculptured horses with their hooves raised high with growing interest and lost count of the number of pieces in the collection and wondered how one family could have acquired so many.

When Jill was sixteen she had stayed at the home with the owner's two youngest children while the parents traveled. In addition to learning how much she loved being with the youngsters, she read a variety of books from their library. Studying the selection of art objects gave her a broad sense of the passion and expertise it took to create these wonders. Years later, the homeowners opened a museum, free to the public, and even though Jill's expertise was in family law, she helped them with some of the legal aspects and found a suitable site to house their growing collections.

7

Tom Daniels's parents graduated from high school, dated through the summer and married when his mother became pregnant with Daniels's older sister. There were no pies cooling on the window sill of their old and deteriorating home, no china service on the worn cupboard shelves with chipped paint, no colorful drapes enhancing the plain window casings. The rolling green hills of rural Wisconsin reaching up to the blue skies filled with puffballs of white clouds provided beauty where very little could be found in their lives. The bluebird's songs filled the fields where there was no other music and the blooming phlox and cornflowers matched the sky, swaying with the gentle summer breezes. His mother made the best of what little they had by sewing Celia's clothes and mending Daniels's ragged jeans until they fell away from the strong patches. Bouquets of native flowers graced the marred wooden table in the kitchen bringing color to an otherwise gray room. A lone picture of Daniels's Grandparents hung on the wall of the small living room. Taped to the back of it was a note "Taken the day George Daniels became President of the Polk County Historical Society."

The quilts on their beds his mother made from scraps garnered from the basement sales at the church they attended once a month for the free potluck dinners. She used a treadle sewing machine given to her by a parishioner who had replaced it with a fancy electric model. Quiet and soft spoken, Helen Daniels tempered sternness with carefully selected compliments. These became the driving force for Daniels to strive to become successful at whatever activity he chose.

Celia at age fourteen took care of Daniels when their mother died of pneumonia. Celia had found her mother, Helen, by the barn, clutching the rope tied to the lone cow they kept for milk. The chickens and the cow became Daniels's refuge from the loneliness and despair he felt with the loss of his mother.

Daniels's father, a salesman, spent weeks at a time traveling and when he came home he didn't speak unless he was angry. After his wife's death, the overstuffed chair in the living room showed wear and a permanent depression where he sat for hours. The table next to it was filled with white rings made by the glasses of whiskey, cooled with ice, put there by Celia at his loud command. Gone were the delicious fried chicken dinners with mashed potatoes and gravy, and fruit pies that the church had provided, and the loving touch by the women in the kitchen who had often given Tom and Celia extra helpings. Gone was the guiding wisdom from his mother, and her attempts to conceal their poverty by her appreciation for the beautiful landscapes offered each day without exacting a cost.

Tom watched his sister take over their mother's duties, pressing down firmly with her hands on the kitchen table to press their father's shirts into acceptable smoothness whenever the electricity was turned off, or warming a can of beans using the large candle with several wicks Helen had made by hand.

Life with their embittered remaining parent became a challenge to seek invisibility. Tom managed to get his father riled without much effort. The belt came off, and he got whacked across the buttocks and back until he begged for forgiveness for the imagined insult.

Celia never came to his rescue, fearing punishment as well. Daniels remembered the times their father did go after her because she would then hunt Daniels down in his hiding place in the barn at the back of the property, and berate him for being stupid enough to get caught doing something wrong.

Tom began writing creative short stories alone in his room. He'd close the door against the barrenness and neediness of his life, allowing his pencil to erase it all, and to create people whose lives he could control.

He wrote stories about families who took trips together, teaching their children to appreciate the wonders surrounding them. Everything lacking in his life came easily to the characters in his prose. He beamed with self-satisfaction when one of his stories was chosen best in his classroom at school.

His father rifled through his papers one day while Tom was tending to the cow.

"What in tarnation is this pap?" he trumpeted when Tom came in through the back door.

Tom took a tenuous step forward to take the papers from his father, noting the glare of marble-hard eyes demanding his request be met with no compromise.

"Oh, no you don't. You're not spending your time writing this crap. Here. Go burn it in the fire."

Tom's mouth opened as if to question his father's demand.

"I said, burn it."

Tom had to obey.

His last memories of Celia were etched in his mind. At fifteen, she became so erratic in her behavior that Tom feared for his life. Happy one day, depressed and volatile the next, it was the time she came at him with a butcher knife that sealed his heart from feeling any emotion connected with her. Just before her sixteenth birthday he watched her through the crack in her bedroom door, packing a bag. She slammed the front door when she left. He never saw her again and he vowed to forget her and the father he had grown to hate.

Tom left home at seventeen, hitchhiking to Texas. He lied about his age and got a job in a warehouse. He worked hard and found the labor enabled him to put his childhood behind him and to become a valuable and indispensable employee. He made friends with everyone. The men became weekly companions at The Last Corral Bar and Restaurant where he decided he wanted to be the life of the party. To be accepted and sought after, he memorized jokes and asked questions to learn his companion's likes and dislikes so he could tease and amuse them. He studied the manner of dress of other bar patrons and began to emulate those he met who held positions of power and trust.

"Just call me Daniels," he told them. He thought it carried a sense of importance. 'Tom' seemed too ordinary.

His tactics worked well. He admired Jack Slade in particular. A visit to Jack's home revealed a cultured man who appreciated art and had been educated in business. Jack proved to be a master at wood carving. He showed Tom his collection one evening.

"You should sell this stuff. It's so well done. You do the staining yourself?"

"Yes. I have boxes of the stuff. Wanna see?"

Daniels's eyes brightened when he saw the intricately carved figures and ideas swirled around in his brain.

"Look. You carve, I'll help stain 'em and I'll sell these. We'll make enough to save up for a place to make and sell more. What do you say?"

"I've been saving up and waiting for the right opportunity. I need a good salesperson. I think we could do well together."

The two worked out a plan. Daniels became immersed in learning how to set up a business with Slade's direction and he began to realize his own potential in sales. He went on the road to get new accounts and used the internet to find other buyers. After many months of selling and finding new ways to get their goods marketed, they rented a warehouse. Daniels began to import other kinds of original art forms. Their shelves overflowed with quaint and unusual artisan carvings that included handmade jewelry, small tables made of exotic woods and renderings of animals from around the world. Orders were coming in every day. As inventory shrank the bank account swelled with enough to buy the building outright. They decided to convert part of the large area to a woodworking shop and hired more carvers and found new sources for the items that were most in demand.

An automobile accident took Jack Slade's life five years later. Daniels's only experience with death had been his mother's and it left him determined to put aside his feelings to deal with the present as he had when she abruptly left his life. He learned that Jack had left his entire portion of ownership to Daniels. Taking over the entire operation proved daunting, but through his burgeoning list of contacts he was able to hire an operations manager who made it possible for Daniels to continue traveling and selling.

In Tucson, Arizona Daniels opened a sales office and he stayed near the area long enough to become friendly with his neighbors. He was often sought after as a dinner guest because of his jokes and friendly disposition.

The business grew and prospered.

At nearby shopping mall he had an opportunity to analyze what kind of items were being offered and which of those showed good sales volumes. It was his way of keeping aware of demand and what he could buy and sell less expensively through wholesaling.

It was there that he met the love of his life by accident while on one of his jaunts to the mall.

8

Tom Daniels and Jill Anderson met by accident at the Mall in Tucson, Arizona. Jill dropped her purse when she was carrying an armful of purchases. Gentleman Tom helped her recover the bags and packages. He thought she was lovely with long blond hair, skinny legs and the sweetest smile radiating out from heavenly blue eyes.

Jill worked at a firm where she became well known for her expertise in family law. She appreciated the lavish attention Daniels showed her. He had a big hearty laugh and she believed his compliments. He told her often she was the most gorgeous woman in the world. They dated steadily for months and married at the courthouse in Tucson.

Daniels owned the wholesale business and had accumulated enough money for them to buy their first house.

Jill continued to work until she became pregnant. Complications arose and she lost the baby in the second month.

Months passed and she became withdrawn and their lovemaking dwindled. Daniels learned to live with her mood swings, hoping they would pass as time went on.

"I think you should make an appointment with a psychologist," he told his morose partner. "We'll have other babies, just give us a chance. I'm sure your firm can recommend someone," he pleaded.

Jill's sour moods disappeared after several months. Her relationship with Tom improved and they began to make more plans for their future.

The Daniels's decided to move to Spartan, Arizona, in the cool climes near the border of a state forest preferring to raise a family in a small town atmosphere. Neighbors were few and located sparsely about their gated community. They built a large home among the towering Douglas firs and spruce trees rising up at the edge of the forest. They added a garage and a sizeable shed where Daniels kept his collection of guns. The upper loft became an office Daniels used for his business.

The next year Jill was ecstatic to find herself pregnant. Their son Porter came a few weeks early and underweight according to prevailing standards for newborns. They had to leave him in the hospital for an extra week. All through childhood he seemed to suffer every illness with drama and severity. Their Nanny complained so often about Porter being too difficult that Jill made the decision to be a stay-at-home mom after many months of unsuccessfully begging the woman to keep trying.

Porter blossomed under his mother's careful nurturing. He remained moody, but his excessive glee at winning children's board games, coupled with hysterical fits when thwarted, seemed irrational in his father's eyes. Daniels's constant scolding about Porter's mood swings placed a wedge between him and Jill.

Two years later Jill gave birth again. They named her Christina.

While growing up, Christina tolerated her brother's moods and antics. They didn't play well together; Porter insisted on winning each game and confiscated every toy. She amused herself and limited the time she spent with him.

Porter graduated from high school at the top of his class and went on to college in Southern Arizona. Porter gravitated toward his mother as Daniels traveled more and more and did not spend time with either child.

Christina became more beautiful each year. Tossing her hair to the side with a flick of her wrist, Christina announced to her parents that she was moving out of their home at sixteen and in with her boyfriend. She dragged her suitcase out the door and into the waiting cab.

Daniels had long ago given up trying to control his independent daughter. He examined his wife's face for some enlightenment, but his eyes were met with a defeated expression. They never discussed her situation again.

9

A year later, Christina called and wondered if her parents would allow her to move into the loft above the shed.

"Why not your old room?" Daniels asked.

"I'd like the privacy," she answered.

Daniels welcomed her arrival.

"What happened to what's his name?" Daniels asked.

"This is really none of your business, Dad, but, let's say he had other rows to hoe," she said without looking up from her dinner plate. "I've learned a lot since I've been gone. I'd like to start helping you with your business."

"Hmmm. I never thought I'd live to see the day. I'd be happy to teach you the ropes. I'm busier than ever, and I could use some help. Let's celebrate." The heirloom heavy cut-crystal whisky glasses were filled with his best Scotch.

"Dad, I think you've been into this stuff most of the afternoon," Christina stated as she listened to his slurred speech. She glanced at her mom, whose eyes pleaded with her to leave the subject alone.

"So. What's that got to do with the price of merchandise," he said. His laughter at his awkward joke became a choking mess of guffaws. Christina went to her father and pounded on his back. Once he got his breath, he walked out the front door and into the woods.

Jill turned away, carrying dishes to the kitchen and Christina joined her.

"Has he been like this long?" she asked her mother.

"Well, yes," Jill hesitated. Ever since, since…"

"Since what, Mom."

"Since Porter…." Jill began.

"I have been too busy since I left home to keep in touch with Porter. What's he done that's so upsetting?" Christina asked.

"You've changed, Christina. You've grown up. I like the change," Jill offered.

"Mom, what's Porter done that upset Dad?" she repeated.

Jill's voice had a sharp edge. "Trouble. Always trouble. After college. He couldn't keep a job. This boy, Diddle, Fiddle, or some such, hounded him on and on. He couldn't deal with the harassment. He had no friends. I persuaded him to get your Uncle John's help. I went down to Tucson many times. Got him out of jail…he acts like a madman sometimes. We paid for counseling; I found a nice house for him to live in…and now," she sighed. "The dog…and the money. It's always about money. And trouble," she answered so loud it made Christina shrink backward.

"Mom. Please, calm down. I had no idea. What's to be done?" she put her arm around Jill's shoulder.

"Nothing. Well, nothing more. We've done all we can. The dog? You've seen the dog?" she continued.

Christina sighed deeply and removed her arm. Her

forehead creased with concern over Jill's inability to stay with one thought.

"The one in the kennel outside? The dog is beautiful, but not friendly. Growls at me," Christina said. "Barks like nothing I've ever heard before." She had decided it was easier to continue the conversation in whatever direction her mother chose.

"He's half wild. Porter loves him, but he didn't give him proper care, so I brought the dog here. Thought the woods would be right for him," Jill explained. "Do you want some dessert? You could call some of your old friends now that you're here."

"Mom, we were discussing Porter. I want to know more," Christina coaxed.

"Porter...oh yes, Porter. Trouble. There's always trouble there. With him. Did you see the dog outside?" she asked, a deep frown creasing her own forehead.

Christina gave Jill a sympathetic look. "I'll wash the dishes, Mom. You go upstairs and read for a while. I'll be going to bed soon, anyway."

"All right, Christina. I like having you here." She smiled at her daughter before she turned toward the stairs.

Christina carefully wiped the dishes and puzzled over the changes in her mother. The soft-spoken, articulate, lover of the justice system lawyer appeared to be lost in a world out of touch with reality. No longer wearing the latest in proper court attire, she now wore drab shirts and jeans with no particular flare. Even her shiny blond hair had become lackluster. Her notable resolve to forge on no matter the circumstance that she'd shown with Porter was slowly giving way to acceptance.

Christina finished the dishes and went outside to find her father. She found him in the shed, looking over his collection of guns and rifles.

"Dad, Mom seems to be getting worse. Did you take her in for an evaluation?" she asked.

Daniels was still slurring his words. "Yes. They can't seem to get the diagnosis straight. Alzheimer's or dementia. I don't know."

Christina noticed tears in his eyes. "Dad, there are plenty of facilities with the right methods to help. Do you want me to make arrangements?"

"No." There was a long thoughtful pause. "I can make more appointments. It hurts to see her like this. I try to keep her on track."

"Well, drinking too much doesn't help or change anything. But you know that."

Daniels glared. "I don't need you telling me what I should or shouldn't do, young lady… Sorry. I'm sorry. I'm always sorry. Not sure I can continue on."

"Dad, let's go back in the house and we'll talk more. Come on." Christina urged her father away from the guns.

10

While Christina worked and lived with their parents, Porter, at twenty busied himself with studies in college. He was better looking than many and tall enough to play basketball. He examined himself in the mirror at the gym. He touched the lines of concern that had formed on his forehead and noted the deep creases by his eyes.

Porter braced himself against the padded leg rests of the exercise equipment. He grabbed the barbell and pushed the weight up, keeping his elbows locked. His face wrinkled up with the effort and he held the bar in place for several seconds. He blew out air with force, breathing in again through his nose to repeat the exercise until the maximum amount of lifts was accomplished.

Workouts at the gym had begun six months earlier. With Uncle John as his psychiatrist and his new diet lower in calories, he had learned the importance of physical health and learning to stay on the regimen. His mental illness felt more controlled than ever. The new medications had fewer side effects than the ones prescribed before and with his workouts at the gym he could see muscles developing in his legs and arms.

Before treatment, confusion and depression had taken over. The voices that had controlled his inappropriate actions seemed banished for now. He understood that if he did not maintain the protocol prescribed by his uncle, he would not be able to keep the demons from filling his mind. He did not wish to fail. The price already paid was too great. He'd been bewildered when he found himself in jail wondering what he could have done to get himself arrested and embarrassed that his mother had traveled several times to Tucson to pay his fines and overdue bills.

When his mind had cleared, he realized that his nemesis, Carson Dittle, knew just how to manipulate him. The thought of him caused Porter to bend his head forward until he was staring at the table. He closed his eyes and began to think about his tormentor. The taunting was hard to forget; the physical attacks even more difficult.

The years of disappointment he'd endured because of his father's lack of compassion or involvement made any kind of relationship with him impossible for Porter to embrace. He had worked hard to become an important member of his debating and basketball teams in high school but Tom never bothered to delay a trip or come home early to attend any matches. His mother was always there and she did her best encouraging him to excel, but the void left by his other parent was too evident to ignore. He had learned to show no emotion when Tom came home, but hated it when he was never questioned about his activities or whether or not he had done well.

Porter stepped onto the treadmill and set the pace higher and then higher still until sweat saturated the band around his head. He ran, speculating as he often did whether or not he could ever exercise enough to get the gut wrenching disappointments out of his system.

Forty minutes of accelerated exercise came to an end. He left the gym after the appropriate cool down period. The stretches slowed his heartbeat and he felt the calm returning to his mind, the walk back to his apartment exhilarating.

11

A year later, Porter now twenty-one, had reached a milestone in his treatment. He and his Uncle John had talked at length about the new life he was about to begin. He was promised exit from the confusing and disappointing world he lived in. It had given him hope, courage and determination to finish what was started. Uncle John had given him permission to spend time in Spartan with his parents.

Porter spent an hour at the gym and then went home. The information he'd been given led him to believe that this day would be the last he would spend in this town and this residence. He went up the stairs to his apartment with purposeful steps. He went straight to his bedroom and pulled a suitcase out from under the bed and filled it with clothing. He decided to pack the personal items after a shower. He expected his Mother to arrive soon to take him to Spartan where he was anxious to be reunited with his half wolf-dog. Anticipating the end of this life put a wide grin on his face. His Uncle John and his sister had made the kind of plans he was anxious to execute. He'd also been assured of freedom from pressures his family placed upon him. *Will my fa-*

ther ever understand why I don't want to spend time with him, once I get back to Spartan?

* * *

When Jill arrived to bring her son home to Spartan, she embraced him and he noted her joy at seeing him.

"It feels good to be here to bring you home and not to get you out of trouble," she said with a laugh. Porter hugged her hard.

"Mom, if I could fix you, I would."

"Fix me. What do you mean? I'm fine. Just fine," she smiled.

They enjoyed the long drive back to Spartan. They chatted about everyday things.

"Your dog howls something awful, Porter. Sometimes I get a shiver down my back."

"He's probably lonesome. Dad ever walk him or play with him?"

"Well, no. He's not too fond of your animal, you know. And he's seemed distracted and... "

"No need to explain, Mom. I get it."

For a few miles they were silent. The forest came into view soon after they passed through Phoenix. Porter turned his eyes toward his mother and smiled. His gaze turned to the scenery outside his window and his thoughts to what he thought lay ahead.

* * *

DANIELS WAITED IN his den anticipating Porter's arrival. He thought back to all the years of financing Porter's treatments. Daniels's frustrations had mounted. Their money had dwindled along with his Jill's short-term memory. She traveled often to Tucson and did her best to minister to Porter's needs to no avail. Each trip was forgotten and replaced with the next, filled with an undying resolve to set things straight. Jill had suggested he drive back with her from Tucson to their home in Spartan and he'd agreed.

Daniels shoved his hands into his pockets while he went over the conversation he'd had earlier in the day with John.

"That boy I told you about is planning something terrible. We have to do something soon," John told Daniels.

"What about now?" Daniels asked.

"Is Jill on her way to get Porter?"

"Yes. They should be back here any minute."

Daniels hung up the phone, sighing heavily.

He walked to the window in the den when he heard the car's tires crunch over the snow-packed driveway. He looked out the window to see Porter lifting his bag from the car's trunk and heard Porter's dog greet him with a long wolf-like howl.

Daniels stared at his boy. He hardly recognized him.

Almost immediately it became evident Porter would not help fill the void left by their daughter. Days passed and he began to slip into depression. He spent hours with his dog, finding solace in the unconditional acceptance given without expectation. He chose not to speak to either his mother or father in anything but simple conversation. Hours of silence would pass.

"How's your lunch, Porter? Can I get you anything else?" his mother inquired. She appeared oblivious to his growing despair.

"Porter, you want to hike the woods with me and your wolf-dog? Fresh air should perk you up," Daniels would try. He knew the answer was 'no', but asked anyway. The three continued to live together, but interaction didn't happen often.

Before dinner, Porter sat in the pen with his dog thinking about his situation. He'd been led to believe by everyone, his father, his uncle, and his sister, that his existence as he'd experienced it was going to be gone, forever. Nothing seemed to be changing. His father drank too much, his mother wafted in and out of reality, and his sister hadn't shown up as she had promised. He felt the old depressions returning and his inability to cope becoming overwhelming.

He wished it to end, permanently.

After dinner he felt his cell phone vibrate. He grabbed a jacket and left the house.

12

Dinner that night seemed no different than what had become their normal routine. They passed the food with no conversation. None of the frequent outbursts occurred from Porter that had become usual when he was a child. Tonight he ate a little; an improvement over eating nothing the past few days.

After dinner, Daniels poured another drink for himself.

"This is only my second, so no words, okay?" he said, looking over at Jill.

"I wasn't planning on saying anything," she said. "By the way, I read your letter to the editor in the paper this morning. Are you sure you want our friends and neighbors to know your political positions? Wouldn't it be better to keep those thoughts within the walls of our home?"

"Home? Home, you say. No one's ever here for me to talk to. You're always with *him*. Not *here*." He took a breath. "I'm sorry, Jill. I don't know what's come over me. All this business with Porter. I can't fix any of it. You can't fix any of it. I'm nearly broke. All the bills to try to get Porter the help he still needs. We can't go on like this much longer."

"Did you feed the dog? I don't think Porter remembers."

His face twisted in frustration and grief. "Please go up to our room now. I'll be up in a while."

Daniels remained in his chair, sipping his drink. *I used to be the life of the party. Now we never go out. I find nothing to get excited about. I'm not the man I was, showing off my beautiful intelligent wife to friends and neighbors. At least my debts will decrease now that Porter is here. But he's not really **here**. Never could talk to that boy. Is it any different?* Daniels head shook back and forth as if the movement would bring an answer. *Soon. It will be over.*

The corners of Daniels mouth drooped downward, his eyes cast down to the floor as self-hatred and disappointments permeated his thoughts.

He sat up straight and brought his mind to the present. *Where did Porter go off to anyway! I'd better see what he's up to.*

13

Much earlier on that day Christina drove to Spartan. The rental car was perfect. Four-wheel drive would get her through any ice or snow. Most of the roads were in excellent driving condition, although blowing snow in some spots could make the drive treacherous. She arrived at The Hitching Post bar and restaurant at the appointed time and found Carson Dittle hunkering down in the alley. She noticed how black his hair appeared, poking out from the knitted brown cap he'd pulled over his ears. His jacket showed heavy wear and the zipper was undone. She couldn't be sure if the flush on his face reflected the cold or was a result of something else. She pushed the button to open her window.

"How long have you been waiting?"

"Maybe an hour. It's friggin' cold out here. You're late."

"No. I'm right on time. Now get in!" She closed her window.

He straightened up and tried to open the passenger side door, but Christina had locked it. She opened the passenger window a crack and informed him he should get in the backseat. She knew better than to have him in the seat beside her. She touched the taser gun hidden next to her right leg, prepared to use it if necessary.

"There's stuff in the bag on the seat. Wear the shirt and put on the jacket that's in there. It's too cold for the one you've got on. And the other, Dittle, use sparingly."

"What's with me in the backseat, Babe? I want to do a little touchy feely while we're motoring."

She heard a rustle of something opening and closing. Then a long slurp.

"In your dreams."

"I'm dreaming now," he said. "Good booze."

Christina turned up the volume on the radio. In the rearview mirror she watched Dittle, his eyes closed, bobbing his head around to the rhythm of the tunes. The warmth of the car's heater and the constant beat of the music lulled Dittle into quiet submission.

Christina felt soothed and her confidence rose. This was going to work okay. Half an hour passed without conversation. A sudden move from the back of the car gave her no time for reaction. The tightening of something against her throat caused her to choke. She accelerated first and then stepped hard on the brake bringing the vehicle to a sudden stop and she pulled the keys from the ignition. Dittle's body flew hard against the back of her seat and then he rocketed into the back. He lost his grip on her neck but not his purpose. He came at her again. Christina fought to gain control. She pressed the button to open her door and fell out onto the snow. Dittle wasted no time in piling himself out and on top of her.

"Babe. Hold still. I just want…"

They struggled for dominance for several minutes. Dittle couldn't manage to control her as Christina continued to wrestle away from him, kicking and scratching. She managed to stun him with a hard punch to his nose. While Dittle wiped the blood beginning to drip, his eyes turned hard and steely and he swung at her. She anticipated it and deftly moved away from the menacing fist. Both of them scrambled back to their feet. He threw another punch that glanced off her shoulder. His boot came up swift and hard. It came perilously close to her chin and grazed her ear. She knew she could finish him, but that would cause an unwanted outcome. She grabbed hold of his boot and threw him to the ground.

"You're damned fast for a friggin' girl! Bitch! Lay off, will you?"

She leaned, grabbed his jacket front and yanked him into standing position. Dittle threw the back of his elbow into her cheek. Christina countered with her knee into his groin. It missed, and landed on his thigh. He flinched and backed away a few inches.

"Now look!" She heaved out her breath as she spoke.

He came at her again. She exhaled loudly as his head hit her square in the stomach. She rose up quickly and nailed his chin with her head. He went down flat on his back in the snow.

She stood upright to look at him for a second and went into a crouch position.

Dittle got up on one elbow and laughed. "You look like you're going to attack me! No, no, Babe. Come 'ere now. Help me up here. Let's make up."

"There's no making up Dittle. Get your sorry ass up and help me find my keys. You stupid, dumb, cringe-worthy creature. Move it! We're on a tight schedule here!"

Dittle scrambled to his feet and used his boots to

move the snow about. "Friggin' hard to see Babe, it's startin' to get dark!"

Christina brushed snow aside in several areas near the car until she found the keys.

She looked at Dittle and saw him breathing hard. "Got 'em. Now get yourself back in the car. We've got some time to make up." *And I've still got the advantage, punk. I've got ammunition you'll never see coming.*

They drove on for another hour and a half, Christina stopped the car at the side of the road. After placing a tiny speaker in her ear for her cell phone and hooking the mic to her lapel, she got out and opened the door. She dragged her unsteady passenger out of the back seat. "Shape up, idiot. You've got to have your best game on for this."

She felt her heart beginning to beat rapidly. She spoke softly. "It's time. Be where I told you." She pressed the remote button at her waist to turn the speaker off.

Dittle smiled. "You have the gun?"

"No stupid. You brought it. In the bag there on the floor. Time for you to learn a few things. Time to get real."

"Yeah! I'm so ready."

"I'll bet you are."

Christina took the out the bag, pulled out the gun, tucked into her jacket and tossed the bag back into the car.

"Go. This way. We're going to do a short practice first. I'll show you where."

She used the time it would take to get to her parent's property to rant about every detail she knew about Dittle. She instructed him to walk in front of her.

"It all started in high school, huh, Dittle. You had no

parents because they couldn't stand the look of you. That protruding forehead, your beady eyes and washed out hair color. You dye it. I know. Lucky for you there was a family that took you in. They couldn't stand you either, but you got out on your own when they'd had enough. I watched you sleeping by the old barn outside of town many times. Didn't know I knew that, huh?"

Dittle turned to Christina and glared.

"I saw you in my bedroom that night, little boy. Pathetic. You didn't even try to touch me. But I know about the girls you did touch. And rape. I have pictures, Dittle. Videos, Dittle. The ones you took of yourself hurting those girls, Dittle. Beating my brother was just a bunch of fun for you. You messed up big time, Dittle. You stole from my uncle. Big mistake."

Dittle turned slightly toward her, his eyes were wide, his mouth open as he listened.

"The Feds are on to you. I gave them every piece of evidence against you. The videos, the pictures, your fingerprints taken from my uncle's computer and file cabinets. You're going away for a very, very long time unless you do exactly what I tell you."

They reached Daniels property in minutes and made their way to a small area by the shed.

The moon was bright as the clouds meandered across the sky passing over it as if turning a light switch on and off. A cold penetrating wind picked up sending shivers down Christine's back. She leaned against the huge bolder, talking softer to Dittle. The yelling at him quit as soon as they passed the Daniels' gate to their property. There was no room for error and she couldn't chance they'd be heard. She felt she had him under control.

"Now, let's practice. Here's where I do you the big fa-vor and you take care of Porter. We have to make sure you do it right." She examined the gun thoroughly and gave it to Dittle.

14

A week after Porter's death Daniels packed a small
duffle bag and went to the dog en to get his dog
Rogue. Porter's dog howled.

"Hush up you friggin' dog. You'll wake the whole
damned neighborhood. He shoved the dog's shoulder
with his boot to keep him from getting out of the pen.
Stay where you belong."

"Come on Rogue, we have work to do. This is a good
day to go. Jill and her brother are busy at the funeral."

Daniels drove his SUV up to the hangar where he
kept his small engine plane. He climbed in, making sure
his dog laid on the blanket he kept for warmth. The flight
would not take long.

He parked his plane in his bother-in-law's hangar at
his home in Tucson, arriving before dawn. It was located
far enough from their house so that they could be certain
no one would be aware of his arrival. He had keys to the
Land Rover that was parked alongside of the building. He
loaded Rogue into the passenger seat and drove slowly
out of the area and into town. They traveled on in the
breaking dawn until he found the area circled on his Tucson city map. He parked a block away from the building.

"Rogue, this is where you do your work." He pulled out a shirt John had procured months ago from the satchel and let the dog get a good whiff of it. "That's right. Fill up those sensors with everything you can. We're gonna find that bastard." The dog sniffed and trembled with excitement in anticipation of the hunt.

The morning sun began to rise out of the eastern sky, warming the air by a few degrees. The row of apartments threw off the cloak of darkness revealing aging facades in need of repair.

"This is the last place Anderson had an address for that kid. And I've got the key he copied. Here you go, Rogue. Up the stairs like a good boy. Now take another sniff."

Daniels went through the hall and up the stairs taking care to be as noiseless as possible with the eager dog beside him. He stopped at the door of the apartment numbered six and paused. He put the key into the lock and turned it. The door opened and he and the dog slipped into the room. The curtains were drawn and it took a moment for his eyes adjust to the darkness. Rogue whined. Daniels quieted him stroking his back.

Daniels and the dog moved through the room until his leg bumped into a piece of furniture. He whispered an expletive. He let his hands guide him to the side of the room where he found another door. It was ajar. He took out a knife from the sheath attached to his belt. There were no curtains covering the windows in the room and the early morning light gave him an unobstructed view. He had expected to find the person he hunted asleep.

The door squeaked as he opened it further. He saw a bed frame with a mattress. He checked the closet. Empty wire hangers clanged together when he pushed them aside. The light from the window illuminated the dust coming up from the floor making rays of silk-like threads in front of him.

Daniels let out an exasperated breath. "Son-of-a-bitch if he's not here!" He led the dog to the bed. "Search!" Rogue jumped on the mattress, sniffed every inch of it, agitated.

Daniels brought the dog back to his side. "Good boy, Rogue. He was here. You proved it." His attention focused on the bare room. He checked the closet again and under the bed. A piece of paper caught his eye. He bent over to retrieve it. It had been folded over many times. Undoing it, Daniels straightened his back when he read it. "Get a gun."

"See Rogue? I knew he did it!"

Daniels' face twisted with disgust and he put the knife back in its sheath as he led his dog out of the apartment. He drove the distance back to John Anderson's property, contemplating his next action. He put the Land Rover in the exact spot he'd found it and made his way to his airplane. Daniels flew far out from the landing strip before he turned north to return home. Sure that John had not heard him arrive or depart he settled back in his seat to finish the flight back to Spartan.

He leaned over and stroked his dog. "We'll find him yet, Rogue. Good boy, Rogue. You and me, we'll see this to the end."

* * *

CHRISTINA WAS PARKED across the street from the apartment where Dittle had lived. She saw her father and his dog go into the building. She waited until he exited and watched as he pulled away. She shook her head as she realized why he must be there and why he hadn't made the trip to go to the funeral.

15

Two weeks had passed after Porter's funeral. Daniels got up from the dinner table and went to the liquor cabinet. He pulled out a bottle of Scotch and poured a double shot into the heavy crystal glass. He held the drink up, turning to Jill.

"Here's to you. Out of a glass from your father's bar, filled with nothing but the best. And I toast you. You're nothing but the best." His twisted expression belied the words he directed toward his wife.

"You've had enough," Jill replied.

Her confused expression, her eyebrows pulling together and eyelids drooping gave Daniels a dose of guilt.

"I'm going to bed. I'll clean up in the morning," she said. Her voice trailed off as quiet as the snow falling outside their enormous picture window as she walked upstairs.

"Okay. I'll put the dishes in the dishwasher, Jill. Like always," he said to the walls of the living room. *Why do I get on her for heaven's sake! She can't help what's happened to her. I need to forget for a while.*

He moved to the cushioned couch with a fresh drink in hand and stared out at the heavy snow accumulating on the bird feeder to the left of the window. He picked up the remote and turned on the fifty-two inch HD TV with the surround-sound volume on high. He enjoyed the experience of feeling like he was in the stands at the basketball game. His interest gave way to booze-induced drowsiness. Soon he snoozed while the broadcast played on.

Jill lay in her bed, propped up with pillows, reading a book. Her eyelids grew heavier and she laid the novel in her lap. Rubbing her eyes gently, she gazed about the room, resting her eyes on her parent's formal portrait. Those days were easier to remember. She closed her eyes for a moment. She remembered the men in dark suits in the library. She had wandered in one afternoon carrying her teddy bear but her father whisked her away and sent her up to her room. She blinked, the memory jolting her from her peaceful reverie. She turned and that scene faded. The wedding picture on top of the dresser caught her attention. Her parents had been apprehensive about her choice of husband, but Daniels had managed to win them over with his wit and charm. Tom had changed; now he was rarely sober, and his temper caused her to flinch and recoil into herself which had become an uneasy and bewildering place to be.

16

A month after the suicide Tom and Jill sat together in the living room of their spacious home quietly reading their newspapers.

"Looks like there is some kind of trouble at Porter's school. I'm glad he is away from there," Jill commented.

"Away. He's as far away as you can get, Jill. For cryin' out loud, he's dead," he exclaimed.

"Yes, I remember. You don't need to shout," she replied, placing her hand on her temple.

Daniels heaved a heavy sigh and returned to the local paper. *I'm still doing it. Getting on her. I've got to stop.*

"By the way, when's the last time you talked to your brother?"

"Oh, he says Porter's treatments are going well, and he's responding to therapy," she answered.

"No. No. I mean, since Porter died," he emphasized. "Has John called? What did he say?"

"Well... I think he told me he's traveling once a month."

"I see. Be sure to let me talk to him next time he calls,"

"Okay. Put one of your notes by the phone for me, please."

* * *

"Hello, John, I'm so happy to hear your voice." Jill said.

"How are you getting along these days?" John Anderson asked of his sister.

"Tom says I'm no worse, but he still gets angry with me, I wish I wasn't like this. My life is so hard," she explained tearfully.

"You keep up with your medicine and you'll be okay. Tom wants the best for you. He cares very much about your wellbeing."

"Oh, wait a minute. Here's a note Tom left for me. I'm supposed to let you talk to him."

"Tom, Tom, pick up the phone, John's calling for you," she shouted.

The phone clicked when Daniels picked up the extension.

"You SOB. Why haven't you called," she listened to Tom, his words exploding with pent up frustration.

Jill hung up the phone, bewilderment creasing her brow.

"What the hell happened?"

"Hold on, Tom. I was shocked. It was a suicide, right? The situation is out of your hands now. Things have a way of taking care of themselves, trust me."

"Right. Trust you. This whole thing isn't what we planned at all. Carson Dittle is still out there. That's just not right," Daniels said.

John was silent for a while. "Look. I'm sorry for your loss, believe me. One day... well... I don't know. You should get on with your life."

Daniels stood holding the telephone away from his ear, his face reddening and a scowl hanging from ear to ear. He slammed the receiver back on the telephone. *Right. Get on with my life. What the hell does he understand about my life?*

17

Daniels spent months going over the circumstances of his son's death. Jill cleaned out Porter's room and laid things out for Daniels to sort through. Among them he found a notebook with stories and poetry written in Porter's hand. All of them interested his father.

Daniels took the notebook to the den. He decided to write a memoir using Porter's experiences. He poured a drink, waiting for the slight feeling of euphoria. That drink led to another and soon he had a brilliant idea.

Writing seemed to clear his head of negativity and evoked some of the feelings of release that his childhood stories had provided for him. He could create a legacy for his family. Days later when a draft had come together, he gathered up the papers.

Looking down at his manuscript, he dialed Sheriff Brown's home number.

"You still writing those western stories, Dennis?" he asked.

"When I get around to it, yes. Why do you ask?"

"I'm working on something. Would like it if you'd take a look."

"Sure. I'll be in my office in town; you can stop by there."

Daniels drove to town and entered the Sheriff's small office. He was nervous in Brown's presence.

He opted to start the conversation with something other than his manuscript. "I've wondered, well actually for some time now. Why haven't we received an autopsy report?" he asked.

"I'm sorry I don't have more information for you," Sheriff Brown replied. "I hounded the medical examiner's office for a report, but... well... they can't find anything containing their findings regarding Porter. I think their inability to produce it is compounded because the body was difficult to identify, except for your firsthand knowledge. The dental records could not be verified, and since those bits of information contribute to what paperwork goes from location to location, someone just plain screwed up. I don't know what else to tell you."

"Pretty damned inefficient, I'd say."

"And I'm sure frustrating for you and your family to not be able to settle everything."

Daniels did not know how to respond, so he changed the subject.

"I heard you write western stories as a hobby. My efforts are not at all similar but I would like to know what you think I can add."

"Why don't you sit down? Brown took the draft in his hands and began thumbing through it. His eyes traveled quickly across the pages. His eyebrows shot up at certain points. Several minutes later he handed the papers back to Daniels.

"Well, I think your writing is worth sharing. Any interest in presenting this to the writer's group I belong to? They will give you a critique and help you to bring your manuscript to its best potential."

"Who else belongs?"

"Mostly town folks. Some you probably know. Marianne Lawler is the chairperson."

"Marianne. Yeah... What the hell was she doing with you the night my son died?"

"Um. Yes. Well, I'm sorry. She's a good friend. Nothing much was going on for me and I was taking her home because she was unable to drive herself. Then I got the emergency call to get up to your place. I didn't have time to drop her off. I'm sure you understand."

"Huh... Guess it's not important, but, she's downright nosy. Anyway, I do think my manuscript is well written. Wouldn't hurt to have some pointers though."

Daniels put his papers into the folder, said his goodbye and went out the back rooms of the building that housed the Sheriff's Department.

* * *

LATER ON THAT Monday, Brown stood in line at the Spartan Foresters Bank on Main Street, wishing he was somewhere else. He thought about his meeting with Daniels.

Daniels looks ordinary enough, isn't the kind of man who stands out in a crowd. Hair is pretty gray. Must be in his late 50's. Wears glasses that look like they're from the 80's. And they're a strong prescription. Makes his eyes appear larger than they really are. Not what you'd call a snappy dresser. I suppose working mostly from home allows you to pay less attention to how you look. He didn't look, well, really healthy. Sorta black under the eyes. And bloodshot. Thought I smelled whiskey on his breath. The narrative style he's created using Porter's memoirs is interesting, although I got the feeling the story he's putting down is fabricated. I really doubt Porter was ever in the country Daniels refers to. Wonder if that is his intent. To romanticize his son's life to make it appear more meaningful. Didn't feel like the right time to ask him if he'd found the gun and turned it over to the medical examiner's office.

Brown brought his attention back to the line of people at the bank.

"Well, if it isn't my friend Marianne Lawler. What brings you out on such a fine day," he asked.

"Fine day, you say. Boy is it ever! Sunshine, no wind to speak of. I'm lovin' it," she answered. "Just getting some cash so I can go to the garage sales. You?"

"Cash. Yup. That's what I'm here for. So, what's new? You still writing those mysteries?"

"Yes, I am. And speaking of mysteries," Marianne lowered her voice to a whisper." Some people are talking about Tom Daniels not going to his son's funeral, and," she emphasized, "the neighbors are saying he and his wife acted weird when they came to the house to pay their respects."

"Everybody deals differently with grief, Marianne. You know that from your own experiences," Brown commented.

"Yes, but, listen. I found out from a neighbor that knows the family well that he's putting together a memoir about his son. He claims he died in a foreign country. No, really. That's what he told them," she explained quietly. "Don't you think you should be looking further into Porter's death?"

"Your imagination is working overtime, dear lady. Maybe that's the way he chooses to remember the unfortunate event."

"Remember, shumember," she replied. "Why not just be honest and tell it like it is."

"Not everyone thinks how you do, Marianne. Tell you what. You keep notes for me and in a few years we'll take them out of your files. Then we'll know if they make sense. Deal?" he said smiling. "Hey, move on up. Mr. Jones is finished with his banking."

"Notes. Yes. I'll be keeping notes," her reply as she moved closer to the clerk's window.

She looks almost like a regular person today. Jeans are blue ones and her jacket's not some eye piercing color! Although, that hair color. Not sure about that. Is that a real color?

* * *

THE FOLLOWING SATURDAY the critique group was in full attendance at the library, when the moderator Larry introduced Daniels. "What brings you here, Tom?" he asked.

"I've always been interested in writing and I would like to read some of the book I'm working on and get the group's opinion," Daniels replied. His voice sounded like a man who was delivering an important speech to hundreds of people who were expecting a major announcement.

"How much is complete?" Larry asked.

"A chapter or two, but I want to understand if I'm off in the right direction. This is, however, well written." His eyes scanned the room for a reaction.

"Fiction or non-fiction?" Larry asked.

"Non-fiction. I've put together a memoir about a family member. He searched the space again as if expecting all of them to rise up in congratulations. "I understand you charge an entry fee of sorts … I gave a check to Dennis for your coffers … and a little extra," he stated, raising his nose toward the ceiling.

Daniels's mouth fell open and he was about to say something else, when Larry interrupted.

"Good. Well, then, let's continue with today's critiques," Larry suggested. "I'll put you on the reading list for later." Daniels sat down, the corners of his mouth pursed with obvious disappointment.

The group continued with their reviews, made suggestions to the writers presenting their works and broke for coffee.

Daniels's turn came last. He gained their attention by clearing his throat.

"I grew up in a small town in western Wisconsin. My grandfather was a man of principal, integrity, and education." His eyes scanned over the audience. He puffed out his chest, satisfied they were informed that he came from highly respected ancestry. He returned to reading his memoir and continued for several minutes.

Well into half an hour of recitation, Daniels had gone beyond the usual time allotted for reading.

"My son Porter was an academic, somewhat introverted, although he organized a rock band in his early college years. He died, accidently, at the beginning of his adult years, in another part of the world."

Daniels surveyed the room and wondered about the frown on Dennis Brown's face.

"His legacy is yet to be learned. In collecting his things, we found an incomplete diary, and we hope to find more. Other papers can tell us what he was studying and will have significant value." He paused. "My daughter, Christina... "

Abruptly, Daniels came to the end of his reading. "This is the draft I've completed so far," he explained.

Members asked him a few questions that he answered until Larry called an end to their meeting.

Marianne approached Dennis Brown and took his arm to pull him aside.

"See? See what I was talking about? Daniels is making up stuff. Did you hear the part about his son dying in a foreign country? What did I tell you the other day?"

"Like I said, Daniel's memoir can serve whatever purpose he wants. Don't you agree?" Brown answered.

"Yes, but, he put on a performance. I watched his chest pump up and out. He really thinks his stuff don't stink!" she added.

Brown and Marianne laughed aloud.

"Maybe if he reads more another time we can get more clues to the real story. I'm positive he is purposely misleading us, Mr. LO," Marianne said.

"You could be right. But for now, you keep all you think is important in your notes, okay, Fancy Pants?"

"Hey. Call me FP, would you? I don't want anyone else knowing what you call me, Mr. LO," she said.

"Uh hum. Me, Mr. Lo, you FP. Got it." Brown chuckled to himself remembering how she designated him

Mr. LO for 'law officer' several years ago when they had first met. Now he was having a difficult time not commenting on the lace-embellished jeans she was sporting. He cocked his head and leaned toward her ear.

"I'd lose that shirt if I was you."

"You're not me."

"Doesn't go with those interesting pants."

Her eyebrows shot up. "Go." She gestured his dismissal with her hand.

He gave a little wave to Marianne and walked toward the exit noticing that she had returned her hair color to its natural graying hue.

Daniels rushed out of the meeting room and caught up with Sheriff Brown.

"Well, what did you think," he asked.

"It's your memoir, Daniels. You're writing what you remember or want to remember. Would that be the case? Any reason why you didn't mention your Father?"

Daniels ignored the observation. "For the relatives who may read it, I felt I needed to make some minor changes."

"Sure. I guess we'll meet again next time," Brown suggested as he left the building.

"Yes." Daniels answered. His smiling expression did not reveal what he thought. *None of his frickin' business how I choose to write this.*

18

Daniels found little time to continue writing the memoir. Without Christina's help, he was often busy keeping track of shipments and placing new orders. He flew to Texas several times to oversee stocking of the large warehouse there. Jill's local doctors had assured him she could manage the house and care for herself while he traveled.

When he returned from one trip, he found an invitation on the table by the front door. Neighbors were having a dinner party.

"I'd like to go," Daniels told Jill.

"We haven't socialized much lately."

"You should wear the red outfit."

"Last time I wore it, the jacket got torn."

"You remember that!"

"You grabbed the sleeve, when … "

"Lost my balance," he interrupted.

"No... You had too much … "

"Leave it alone, Jill!"

The Fall evening's cool breezes rushed through the front door of the Barnes' home as it opened for each of the invited guests.

The host, Jack Barnes moved among them, taking part in the animated conversations. The guests were dressed in suits and evening wear holding their mixed drinks with one hand and juggling canapés with the other.

Jack circulated among the twenty friends and found Tom Daniels standing along at the side of the room.

"How's things going with your business?" Jack asked.

"Busier than usual … you know, Porter's living a … "

The abrupt change in subject surprised Barnes. "You mean, in heaven?"

"No … No. Away from the devil."

Jack caught the slur in Daniels speech. "Oh. Same thing."

"You don't get it."

"Been a tough time for you and Jill. Take it easy with the booze Tom. You're going to want to be in shape for poker after dinner, right?"

"Oh. Yes. *In shape*," he emphasized.

Later at the dinner table, Jill glanced over at Tom whose face had turned an ashen color.

"Tom, are you all right?"

"Wush happening!" He clutched the tablecloth, pitched backwards on his chair causing both to hit the floor. His eyes rolled up showing the whites.

The room became filled with the din of broking china until an uncomfortable silence took its place. The dinner guests were stunned.

Jack Barnes called an ambulance. The paramedics rushed Daniels to the hospital. Barnes' wife, Lucy, drove Jill in their car. Jill sat in ashamed silence.

Daniel's lab tests revealed liver damage.

"Doctor says I have to cut down on my drinking, Jill.

I could lose some weight too."

"I'll cook healthier meals. It will be better for both of us."

They never discussed the incident at the dinner party. Daniels took the rest of his alcohol out of the liquor cabinet in the dining room and put it in a file drawer in his office.

19

Winter roared back into the high country of North-ern Arizona threatening to dump record amounts of snow in the region. Tom Daniels had his hands full, caring for his wife and clearing the long driveway and paths on their large property.

Daniels trudged up to the shed where the loft above served as his office, clearing the path as he went. He passed the large kennel looking at its occupants. His dog Rogue seemed to smile back at him.

"What are you lookin' at, devil dog," he said to the other dog belonging to Porter. "You're nothing but a half-breed wolf eating me out of house and home." The dog's howling response gave him a shiver. He turned and con-tinued shoveling, throwing the snow to his right as if the action would make the howling stop.

The phone in his pocket was ringing as he entered the office.

"Hello," he shouted.

"Dad, it's Christina. I've got a long weekend coming up next month. You up for a visit?" she asked.

"Yes!"

"You're hollering."

"No. Can't hear myself think."

"What's that supposed to mean?"

"Never mind. Of course. You can only stay the weekend? Your mother would love the company. I haven't had much time for myself."

"I'll be there Friday the end of next month, Dad."

"Friday. What time did you say?"

Silence. The connection was gone.

He reached over, opened the file cabinet, and pulled out a bottle of vodka.

* * *

THE MIGHTY MOOSE CAFE and Readery in Spartan experienced an unexpected rush of customers early that Saturday morning. Sheriff Brown, his rump firmly planted on a stool at the counter and drinking his coffee, listened to the townspeople talk out their frustrations with others or welcome the warmer springtime breezes christening the wooded slopes. He had no complaints. His stool rotated back and forth as he entertained anyone who would listen with his stories.

The room smelled rich with the mixed aromas of coffee, tea steeping, and the fruit pies baking for the dinner crowd.

"Sheriff Brown. Why did I figure you'd be here on a day like today?"

He turned to see a tall lithesome young woman.

"Well, if it isn't Christina Daniels all grown up," he said smiling at her. *She's a really good looking young woman. Takes after her mother.*

"Yes. All grown up."

91

"I thought you were living in sunny California. What brings you to Spartan?" he asked.

"I had some time off coming from work and decided to visit Mom and Dad. After all that's happened, I figured I needed to show up now and then," she offered.

"Tell me, Christina. How are things with your folks?"

"You ask a hard question Sheriff," she replied, seating herself beside him and ordering a cup coffee.

She paused, a thoughtful, faraway look in her eyes before giving an answer. "My parents are good people, but, well, they never talked to us kids much growing up." She turned on the stool and sipped her coffee.

"Porter was temperamental, you know, and me, Dad just couldn't seem to care enough to find out what kind of person I was or wanted to be."

"I'm wondering how you think they're handling your brother's death."

"They're not. They had Porter cremated almost immediately. I was upset that I didn't have a chance to say my goodbyes. Dad said his face was gone; nothing for me to see. You know Mom's memory is deteriorating, beginning Alzheimer's, so she doesn't always get that Porter's not around anymore. And, Dad wouldn't go to the funeral. Mom had to make all the arrangements on her own, although I helped as much as I could, and so did my Uncle John. I just don't get where Dad's coming from sometimes. Don't get me wrong, if I needed money or anything, all I had to do was ask. But talk about stuff? Uh-uh. Doesn't happen. I learned real quick to figure things out on my own," Christina explained.

"On your own, huh. You seem to be doing all right. What kind of work do you do in California?"

"I'm employed by a company to figure out who, why, or if anyone is hacking into their confidential files. It's pretty interesting. My skills came in handy when I need-ed to check out a dude who was giving me major prob-lems. You need information about anyone, get in touch. I'm your gal."

"You don't say. I'll keep you in mind. Good to see you, Christina. Enjoy your visit. You'll find a lot of snow still up there at your folks place."

Brown excused himself and left the cafe. As he head-ed for his office, he wondered about all that Christina Daniels had shared. *There's a lot more to that girl than she lets on.* Judging by her clothes and manner, he doubted that a California college had taught her the skills to do the job she claimed to be employed at. *Lets on like she's being sraightforward.* He knew that computer hacking and finding those that do it would have required special-ized training.

* * *

BACK AT HIS OFFICE, he'd been on hold for twenty min-utes when the clerk at the Phoenix facility came back on the line.

"Sheriff Brown? I'm sorry to keep you waiting. We have not received an autopsy report for the vic Porter Daniels. I'm going to fax all the data we keep on file to you now. I hope you will find the information helpful," she explained.

Brown waited several minutes until the fax ma-chine chirped and began transmitting the data. He read through it as the papers spilled off the tray.

"Dr. John Anderson, Psychiatrist of Tucson, Arizona confirmed schizophrenic diagnosis, patient name Porter John Daniels age twenty-one."

Brown dialed the phone number on the sheet. "Dr. John Anderson, please. Yes, I'll wait." There was a pause. "This is Sheriff Dennis Brown of Coconino County, office in Spartan, Arizona. I wish to speak to him regarding a former patient of his who is now deceased."

Brown waited several more minutes until his call was answered by Dr. Anderson.

He explained his business and made an appointment for the following week.

"By the way, Doctor, I haven't been in the Tucson area for quite some time. I'd like to bring my horse along, and wondered if you could suggest any places nearby to ride."

"Matter of fact, I own a large piece of land good for riding adjacent to our home. We'll discuss it when you arrive," Anderson offered.

Brown headed back to his ranch early that afternoon, hoping to get a ride in before sunset. As he drove slowly down main street he smiled to himself as he viewed the small town, with its brick-front buildings still emblazoned with the logos of businesses long gone, replaced by quaint shops, art galleries, antique stores, and the hardware store he had turned over to his son when elected Sheriff.

Once on the county roads, his demeanor changed as he thought about his conversation with Christina. *She's a smart gal. Looks you straight in the eyes, as if she wants you to think there's nothing to hide. Her speech doesn't reflect that California sound you get from young people. Definitely educated, but somewhere else.*

He pulled up to his barn. Brown led his horse, Chief, in from the pasture, saddled up and took a ride. The clean air, crisp and chilly, invigorated both of them and the pace picked up before they trotted toward the hills spreading out and upward into the forest. Chief slowed as they began the ascent. Brown was unsure how far they could venture without things getting too slick and sloppy from the melting snows.

At the crest of the first hill, he came to a flat area that had a long paved road that came to a 'T' at the far end. To his right, he observed an outbuilding with huge doors on one side, resembling the airplane hangars he had seen out at the county fairgrounds. Puzzled, he kept Chief still for several minutes thinking. He had never been to this section before. *This must be the new area folks talked about over coffee, the "clearing on top".*

He rode closer to assess the recently excavated piece and dismounted. He tied the sturdy gelding to a nearby tree, then headed toward the building. He tried the side door and found it open. He went inside noting the cleanliness of the large open space. Two Cessna 182 turbo-charged airplanes filled up the majority of it. Brown peered into the interior of the closest one, seeing it was as clean as a freshly detailed automobile. He paused at the wall containing several shelves and closed cupboards. He realized he was on the Daniels's property. He recognized some of the merchandise Daniels exported for his business. The airplanes must be used for his many purchasing trips. The large set of cabinets on the left wall was locked. The table below them had several amber-colored prescription drug bottles setting inside a bin. He pulled a small spiral notebook from the pocket of his leather riding vest and wrote down the names on the containers. As he turned away, his eyes focused on a note on the floor. He picked it up and ran his finger over the strip that had lost its sticky quality. Handwritten in pencil on the right side it read, "John, these don't go."

A large round lidded barrel stood in the corner by the cabinets. Brown lifted the lid and found it filled to the brim with men's heavy winter garments.

Brown's face was stern and thoughtful as he exited the hangar. He untied Chief, unhooked the lead rope and fastened it into place with a leather strap, then grabbed the reins and mounted in one continuous movement.

"Come on, boy," he said as he gently encouraged Chief with the heel of his boot. "We've got some investigatin' to do." To the right of the large building, Brown noticed a "Private – No Trespassing" sign.

The ride home took less time than the slow pace he'd set earlier. Brown unsaddled Chief and left him in the corral and then went inside his house. He fixed a sandwich for supper and sat down at the kitchen table. Looking out over the field, he noticed growth of grasses his horse would soon be nibbling. The cell phone rang.

"Jake. Speak up. I can hardly hear you."

"Sorry. Big pool game going on. Boys are whoopin' it up. Listen, Tom Daniels is here. He's not good. You should come and talk to him or something. There's no cab available tonight, so I can't call for one."

"I'm on my way." Brown wrapped his unfinished sandwich, put on his uniform cap and got into the Sheriff vehicle and sped out of his driveway.

The one cab available in town could be called on Friday and Saturday nights when the bars served the most customers. Any other night, Brown filled in unless he'd been called away because of a serious incident. He figured the driver must be busy with other customers.

He arrived at The Hitching Post, located at the far edge of downtown. It had been established back in the 1800's when loggers came to town for food, drink and lodging. It was one of the last of businesses that served liquor in downtown Spartan. The owner preferred to keep the original minimal decor. Relics of logging tools hung on the walls. Some of those nails were nearly as old as the object that hung on the wall. The pungent intermingling odors of beer, onions and hamburgers permeated the air.

Brown nodded to the bartender, Jake, as he walked by the booths and the tractor seats mounted on boards bolted to the floor. Vintage stools lined the long oak bar, Early American tables and chairs provided a place to eat gigantic juicy cheeseburgers and fries, and wood benches rimmed the wall by the pool table. He spotted Daniels at the end of the bar.

"Jake tells me you need a ride home, Tom."

"Right. Home. Nobody there."

"Ready to go now?"

"Let me think. No... I have a drink to finish."

Brown didn't reply right away, choosing instead to have a look at Daniels, noting his flushed cheeks and wandering focus.

"You know, I gotta tell you, Brown. You have no idea what it's like. Living with someone who's nuts. Mental illness. I can't, I can't deal with people like that. Why can't they just get their head outta their ass and get a life! Am I a horrible person for feeling like that?"

"Not horrible, no, Daniels. Some of us aren't equipped to be..."

"Yes. Like my wife. She has no problem stepping in and taking care of people like that. I can't do it."

"Doesn't mean you don't love them."

"No. No. You don't understand. I couldn' love my sister. Sheez was nuts."

Brown took Daniels' arm and steadied him while easing him off the stool.

"My brother-in-law and me, we made plans. Good plans. Didin' work out. But the devil will be dead, I'm tellin' you."

"Tom, I've got your jacket. Let's us boys meander out of here, out of everybody's sight, okay? The back door's here. I'll help you, oops... this way." Brown guided the wobbly Daniels to the car and helped him to get in.

"Shmy fault the boy's dead."

"How's that?"

"Itzin the family, that's why."

"You're telling me ... "

"I'm tellin' you I fired the cannons that made him sick like that."

"An interesting way to put it."

The ride became silent for a few miles.

"I'm gonna kill 'im, you know. Guess I shouldn' be tellin' you."

Brown glanced to the side. Daniels face was frozen in a sneer.

Quiet enveloped the car once more until they arrived at Daniels' home.

He managed to help Tom into the house with some difficulty.

"God damned empty house! Jush steer me to the couch."

"Where's your wife, Tom?"

"Uh. Left today. Christina too. Tucson. Her brother's. That god damned screw-up."

Daniels passed out when his head met the pillowed arm of the sofa.

20

The next week in the cool early dawn, Sheriff Brown led his horse Chief out of his stall and into the trailer he hitched onto his Bronco. He gave a gentle shove to the back end of his horse and closed the door, checking the latch to be sure it was secure. He got into the truck, pulled on the left turn signal, and found everything was in working order. He did the same for the right signal. Brown started his trip to Tucson, Arizona for his appointment with Dr. John Anderson hoping to get answers to the questions rolling around in his mind.

He had filled his briefcase with documents and a list of the questions he wished to ask. He knew he had little reason to suspect anything, but certain things kept popping up that he wanted to either verify, or put them aside as having no validity.

He had programmed Anderson's address in his outdated Tonto GPS. To his surprise, the GPS's instructions were correct and he arrived at the outskirts of town where Anderson had told him he would find his office and home. Brown located some ironwood trees. He maneuvered his vehicle and horse trailer under their shade and got out and reassured his animal that he would be shielded from the sun. Early morning warmth enveloped him immediately.

Anderson came into the office with a cheerful smile, dressed in a short-sleeved shirt and dress pants. His shoes appeared to be expensive and were polished to a high gloss. Brown wondered when he'd last polished his own worn cowboy boots. The two shook hands.

"Please. Have a seat." Anderson directed him to a deeply tufted leather armless chair in front of his desk.

"I'm curious, Dennis ... Is it all right if I call you Dennis?" he asked. "Is this official business?"

"Not official, Dr. Anderson. Dennis is fine. Conversations with Tom Daniels and his daughter raised a few questions and I thought I should make some inquiries. Please tell me about Porter, his friends, did he have enemies or persons who he thought disliked him? Was he suicidal while under your care? Close with his family? I want to get a better idea of what led up to his death."

"I see." Anderson began to answer the questions. "Porter was a very bright young man. His mental illness, bipolar disorder, appeared in his late teens. When his behavior became problematic, his mother requested I see him, since he attended school nearby. It was a trying time for everyone involved. I would quantify an old high school acquaintance as an enemy who bullied him in ways no one should have to endure and it took a toll.

"Can you identify the bully?"

"He was also a patient of mine, but is no longer. He came in and demanded all his files from me and told me he was going to "disappear" as he put it. I can't give you his name, patient confidentiality you understand. I learned in the last year that he was quite a nuisance, if that's the right word, to my niece, Christina, as well. I remember noting in his file that he could be a danger to himself as well as others. I did what I could for him. I can tell you he wasn't of sound mind the last time I saw him."

"So Porter did have an enemy of sorts. And what you've told me seems to go far in explaining Porter's state of mind. What about his parents; were they close?"

"He was very close to his mother and upset with her diagnosis of Alzheimer's disease. He and his sister were not chummy, but both exhibit family loyalty. He and his father never got along well. I think Tom distanced himself when Porter was young. He couldn't tolerate the tantrums. I know for fact Christina tried to stop the bullying, but it didn't seem to make a difference."

"What kind of medications was he taking? I assume you would have prescribed them."

Anderson hesitated for a second. "I'm not sure this kind of information will be of any help to you."

"It's my inquiring mind. I am interested in all of it, the meds, his family and how they got along. You know, you work with these sort of things."

Anderson stared at Brown for several seconds, then stared down at his desk. He picked up his pen and wrote down what Brown requested. The sheriff slipped the list into his pocket inside the small notebook.

"What would you describe as progress, or lack of it, by the time he went to visit his parents?"

"He was doing very well, actually.

Brown saw that Anderson had relaxed again. "I was sure we had him on the right medications and that his state of mind was hopeful. I don't know what happened in the last month of his life. After the funeral, Jill told me he'd quit communicating, hardly ate and seemed very depressed. They should've alerted me right away but for some reason they didn't. Very sad. His death might have been prevented."

"By the way, Tom mentioned Jill is with you. He has told me about her diagnosis. How is she doing?"

Startled by the question, Anderson's expression changed.

"Well, you see, she's very close with the wife and myself. I believe the transition to our calm surrounding is to her benefit and she is showing no new memory lapses."

"Glad to hear it. I'm sure your steady influence has helped."

"We can only hope for the best for her."

"And Christina? Is she still here?"

"No. She had to get back to work."

"Where is it that she works?"

"Christina is a very private person. We keep in touch, but I don't pry."

"I see. Well. I've taken up enough of your time. I should be going. I thank you for giving me a much better picture of the circumstances. I appreciate it. Brown stood up from his chair, and then turned back to Anderson. "I'll be staying the night in town. Can you recommend a place where my horse and I would be comfortable?"

"You wanted to ride, I remember. Go ahead and take your horse out on my land out yonder." He pointed out the office window. "It's a great day to ride." He made some notes on his business card and handed them to Brown.

"Thanks for the info. I'll call for directions to the motel, and I'll take you up on the offer to ride on your property. Care to join me?"

"I can't this morning. I have appointments sched-uled until late this afternoon," he said looking down at his desk where Brown could see the calendar there filled with notations in each time slot.

Brown walked to his truck mulling over the infor-mation. *Seems like he's pretty honest. But his hesitation at certain points makes me wonder. He could have shed more light on this than he did.*

* * *

CHIEF NODDED HIS HEAD up and down as Brown backed him out of the trailer. He led him to the huge bucket of water he'd filled from the hose attached to Anderson's ga-rage. While the horse drank he went to the cab of the truck and took out an apple. He cut it with his pocket-knife, moved close in to the horse, blew his breath into its nostrils and held out the apple in the palm of his hand for Chief to grasp with his teeth.

Brown saddled the horse and took him slowly out into the desert area for a leisurely ride. The terrain was new to Chief and the horse's nostrils and ears were on high alert for anything resembling a threat. Brown knew it was too early for the snakes to be out of hibernation, so he wasn't concerned with their safety. A slow rise led the two to an area that overlooked Anderson's home. A slight breeze cooled the air as they rode past several saguaros and prickly pear cactus. A sandy road seemed the easiest way to ride and it led them up further onto a plateau. Brown stopped the horse and surveyed the ex-panse. It was quiet. Little puffs of sand twirled off in the distance resembling a mini tornado. He watched them move across the land as they changed direction several times.

He pushed in with his heels and urged the horse to move on. The road widened onto a smooth area of hardened sand, called caliche. Brown had friends who mixed it with Portland cement for construction purposes. There was a large T at the end of the road and a hangar. *Good use of this kind of soil, I'd say.*

Brown pushed his hat back off his forehead, his eyebrows raised. "Well I'll be. Another flyer in the family."

He rode up to the hangar, dismounted and went inside. He was surprised to see a building nearly identical to the one on Daniels's property. Upon reflection, he surmised they probably shared the plans to build it, since they obviously shared an interest in flying. There was one plane inside, similar to one of the two he'd seen in Daniels's hangar. This time he noted the markings on the side of the plane into his notebook.

Brown got back on the horse and convinced Chief to move a bit faster as he was anxious to get to town to do more research and to secure his lodging for the night.

* * *

Brown found the motel Anderson had suggested. He asked the manager where he could board his horse for the night, and found accommodations for Chief a few miles away. That settled, he washed up and set out for the library.

He stood outside the impressive building and admired the six pillars and the beautiful cement carvings that graced the roofline. Upon entering, he read the plaque that told how the original building was built in 1883 and was the first public library in the area. More recently it came under the county's management and was named the Pima County Public Library.

He settled in at a long oak desk after requesting to view the local newspaper for the past three years. It was 5:00 PM before he came upon an article that interested him. It was about a twenty-year old student who had been arrested for stalking and harassing female students at the college. The student's name was listed as Carson Dittle. *There's a name I wouldn't want my kid to have.* He studied the picture alongside the article and was struck by the similarities the boy had with Porter Daniels. There was a head shot, and a surveillance still that showed the boys to be about the same height and build. The article went on to say that Dittle had a long history of trouble with the law, mostly minor infractions, but nevertheless it documented a pattern of behavior problems. *This could be the patient Anderson referred to.*

Later issues of the newspaper reported that Dittle had skipped his court date and authorities were unable to locate him. *That seems to fit with what Anderson told me - his leaving or, what was it. Oh yes. "Disappearing". Sounds to me like the type of person who was harassing Porter and Christina. She did mention to me someone was bothering her in school and she used her computer skills to help stop the problem.*

Brown inquired as to how he could make a copy of the articles and a librarian's aide made it possible. He put the copies into his briefcase and left the air-conditioned facility to head to a nearby restaurant he'd spotted on the way to the library.

The motel was a welcomed sight as Brown pulled in. He felt full from the hamburger basket he'd ordered and tired from the long day. His snores filled the room as soon as he laid his head on the pillow.

* * *

The next morning, before heading back to Spartan, the Sheriff visited the main police station. The Tucson police were cordial and helpful. Brown made it clear he only wanted to get a better picture of what had caused young Porter to take his life. They confirmed what Brown had learned at the library and added what they knew to his information on Carson Dittle.

* * *

Brown's second trip to the library focused on flight information. He had hoped to find documentation on where John Anderson and Tom Daniels frequently flew.

He found a newly developed web site AFSS - Automated Flight Service Station that they may have used to get weather information as well as a flight plan form to fill out. Brown resorted to using the media contact phone number to get to a live person. He was directed to a supervisor. He was not able to find any flight plan filings for Anderson, but there were regularly filed documents for Daniels flying to one destination in Texas.

"No one with a private pilot license has to file a flight plan if following Visual Flight Rules, or Instrument Flight Rules. Using either, weather in Arizona would be ideal for short flights within the state for private aircraft, with the exception of winter storm activity in the northern regions," the supervisor informed him.

Brown checked the notes he had taken in Daniels's airplane hangar. The items he had found stored in the cabinets had had labels with an address of a wholesale outfit located in Waco, Texas. *Looks like his flights were business-related. That leaves Anderson flying about with no record of his. The second plane I saw in Daniels's hangar does belong to Anderson. The numbers I saw on his plane in Tucson match. Does he fly up to Spartan to see Daniels often? He made no mention of it.*

21

Sheriff Brown's home telephone was ringing in the kitchen as soon as he walked in the door after returning from Tucson.

"Hello. Oh, it's you, FP. You sure let the phone ring enough times," he joked.

"I … let … the phone ring? It's your phone, silly. One never knows where one will find you on that ranch of yours, and, heaven forbid you should get an answering machine. What if it was an emergency?" she asked.

"That's what 911 is for."

"Oh. Yes. That's right. 911."

"And the point of your call?"

"Dinner. I have ribs on. Been cooking all day. Want to come over?"

"Did you drain off all the fat? I can't be eating fatty stuff you know."

"Put my special barbecue sauce on them, too."

After he agreed to go over, they discussed the time for him to arrive.

"Mr. LO."

"Yes?"

"Don't be foolin' around so much you forget to come."

"Yes, FP. I'll be there FP. On time, FP. Bye FP."

Brown had a soft spot for the old woman who had come to his front porch many years ago looking for advice about people and happenings in the area. He liked her company, found her nosiness amusing, and it was easy to talk to a woman who was too old for him to think of in romantic terms.

Oh boy. Barbecued ribs. That's gonna be great! He sat down on his rocker, closed his eyes, and fell asleep.

* * *

THE SCREEN DOOR was closed but the front door wide open when he arrived at Marianne Lawler's home. He held on to the bottle of wine he brought with him and stared at the cat looking back at him through the screen door.

"FP. Come and get what's his name. He looks like he doesn't want me to come in," he shouted.

Marianne appeared dressed in a hot pink outfit that made Brown's eyes open wide. "Holy cow! You shouldn't have dressed up for me," he exclaimed. "And don't let that cat get on me, got it?"

Marianne sighed, picked up the cat and smiled at her guest as she opened the door. It's Tangle. And he won't bother you. I've trained him. What's that you've got?"

"I brought red wine. I don't know, is it supposed to be white with ribs?"

"Depends if it's pork or beef. But never mind. Any wine is good wine Mr. Lo. You don't like my outfit? I just finished making the shirt this morning."

"Nice. It's nice. But … well, it's really bright."

"And?"

"Okay. You look terrific. Happy?"

"Yes. I guess."

"Wow. It smells great in here," Brown said as he put the wine bottle on the kitchen counter.

"Ribs the way you like 'em, Mr. LO. Cooked the fat out, drained 'em and put 'em back in the oven nice and slow with the sauce atop. Should be mighty good!"

Marianne put her cat Tangle on his high perch where he could keep a look out for anything needing his attention.

The table was set with dinnerware and utensils and she invited Brown to join her.

"What's that you've got there, FP?"

"A bib, so you can mop up."

"I see. Good idea."

Brown raised his wine glass and made a toast to the cook. He set the glass down on the edge of his spoon and the glass tipped enough to spill some on the tablecloth.

"Oh, sorry!"

"Not to worry Mr. LO. Just drink responsibly. You know what that means, don't you?"

"Uh. Well, of course. Not too much of a good thing."

"Nope. Means don't spill any."

"Got it."

Conversation became limited to 'umm good' and 'more please' until both were satisfied they'd consumed enough.

"Mighty good dinner. I'll take a cold glass of water to settle it down, if you would."

Once they had cleared the table, Dennis helped Marianne put the dishes in the dishwasher. "You'll make someone a good partner, you know," she commented.

"We don't go there, remember?"

"Not going. Just idly commenting. So how come you weren't home yesterday and this morning?"

"Checking up on me?"

"No, but …"

"I was in Tucson getting information about some things."

"Sheriff-type things?"

"Not exactly."

"You're a wealth of information, Mr. Lo. Spill."

"FP, you know our agreement. Nothing that comes out of my mouth can be quoted, referred to, whispered etc. etc."

"Yes. I know. No need to remind this old lady. I can keep it and never repeat it. But discussing stuff is healthier than letting it run amok in your brain."

They took their filled water glasses to the living room.

A loud thump indicated Tangle had jumped down from his perch.

"The cat."

"He's not looking for you Mr. LO. It's me he wants."

"Yesterday was interesting. I learned some things I didn't know. I went to see Porter Daniels's psychiatrist. He's Jill's brother, Porter's uncle. Did you know that?"

She shook her head.

"There's a boy, well, student I think may be an important factor in Porter's death. He has a criminal record and apparently he bothered Christina too. Other than that, not much else to tell."

Marianne was quiet, stroking her cat's back while she thought.

"What important factor?"

"Nothing I can nail down just yet. But it's pretty clear he did contribute to Porter's mental instability."

"I still say Daniels has something to hide."

"He may. You know, everybody deals with things in their own way. I can't speak for Daniels, but I remember how I was when Lizzy died. I really didn't want to go over it with anybody. At all. I was even pretty rude to you," he said.

"But, I understood your grief, and I was devastated by her illness and death too, Mr. LO," Marianne said.

"Yes. Well, let's leave that be," Dennis suggested.

Marianne recognized the haze that came over Dennis's eyes that meant it was time to keep quiet. She waited several minutes to ask another question.

"What did Porter's autopsy reveal?" she asked.

"As far as I know, we haven't received a report to date."

"What? It's been so long!"

"Stuff happens, Marianne. Things get lost, misplaced, the labs are overworked and understaffed, and DNA testing in some places is not as sophisticated as we've been led to believe. The backlog is horrendous!"

"Is it like that everywhere?" she asked.

"Probably not. And things are improving. But, nevertheless, there was no reason to think that anything was any different than what Daniels told us at the time."

"So, you saw Porter's body. Was it awful?"

"Death other than natural causes can be disturbing, at the very least. His face was unrecognizable; it was shot away," Dennis answered.

"Oh, my. Glad I didn't see it."

"I'm thankful you didn't see it. I've been meaning to

ask you. Why did I have to pick you up at the same bar the same time as year before last?" he asked.

"Oh. Well," she started after a long pause. "I don't seem to be able to get past that date very easily. It's the anniversary, of, well, you said you knew about it, after you read the account of the accident on the internet," she answered.

"Right. I didn't put that together. I'm always happy to give you a ride home, you know, but my position dictates that I should not have anyone from the general public in my vehicle when I'm out on official business."

"I'm so sorry to have put you in that position. I didn't want to call that stupid cab driver, he won't pick me up when he finds out how far he has to drive to get me home. Doesn't want to miss all the fares he gets from the tourists at the bar!"

"Really! Not good for the locals. The bar keep told me you sit in the booth by yourself, and get gigglier with each drink, and start to sing!? What's with that! Most people react to booze by getting depressed."

"Yes. Exactly. I get happy. That's the point!" Marianne answered.

An uncomfortable quiet crept into the room like a suppressed memory trying to make its way into conscious thinking.

"Could Daniels be the one who killed Porter and made it look like suicide?" Marianne asked.

"That's one to keep in your notes. Sure, I guess it's possible. Puzzles have pieces. I'm still collecting."

"So you do think something is fishy."

"It's very possible. It is just as possible that there is absolutely nothing fishy."

"I'm sticking with fishy."

"You do that."

"Maybe Daniels is out trying to get evidence against this boy you mentioned."

"Maybe. Doubtful, but again, possible."

"I think you could go over conversations you've had with Daniels and see what he may have let slip."

"Another good idea."

"I heard he's been seen out drinking, to excess, I might add."

"Your ears must be full up by now."

"They are cavernous wells waiting to be filled."

"I should have known."

"Keep aware. That's what I'm suggesting. I know things are not what they seem with that family."

Sheriff Brown's thoughts turned to the airplanes, the clothing, and the prescriptions. "I'm still working on it."

"Good."

On his way home, he mulled over the information he had. What he'd learned about flight regulations regarding personal aircraft flights had not given him any new leads to follow. *Were those prescriptions for Porter or could they be Jill's? What actually caused the young man to take his life? What about the lab where DNA would have been sent? Did they receive it and when? Why does Daniels seem to be putting out information for relatives to read that is not accurate? He's not a stupid person. There must be reasoning behind it. FP has a point. Some things are adding up to something fishy. I would much rather it didn't.*

22

For the love of whatever, Jill, why didn't you tell me your brother was coming?" Daniels hung up the telephone with a look of disdain, brushing crumbs from his breakfast toast off of the front of his jeans. "He's at my hangar, now, expecting me to be there to pick him up."

"I'm sorry. I didn't write it down like I should have. Anyway, it's only a few minutes from here. I'm sure John won't mind waiting," she replied.

Daniels slammed his coffee cup onto the kitchen counter, spilling it and then hurried to wipe off his hands. He grabbed his keys and sped out the front door.

Ever since Jill's return from her visit to Tucson, he'd been irritated with everything she did and said. "Some day. Some day I'm gonna have peace in my life!"

At the Daniels's private hangar Dr. John Anderson fiddled with the keys in his pocket while he waited for his brother-in-law to arrive. He ran his hand over his freshly-shaved cheek while his thoughts rambled.

"I've got to sort some of this out with Tom. Somehow. Without telling him too much. It's been a year. I have to tell him something,"

He glanced up at the sound of the door to the hangar

opening and watched as Tom approached him. *He looks old and haggard. This has cost him.*

"So, you finally show up, you bastard. It's been a whole year," he said to John.

"Hold on, Tom. We'll talk at your place," John suggested.

Once they were in the privacy of his office in the upstairs of the shed, Daniels began his rant.

"Here we are together, finally. What the hell, John. You promised me you had everything under control. You said you located that bastard Dittle and took care of him. But *no*," he began.

"Hold your horses, here. For God's sake, calm down. Your face is red, you're perspiring, and you're going to stroke out if you don't settle down. Now sit," John commanded.

He took Tom by the arm and led him to the leather lounge chair at the side of the room. He pulled up a straight chair, sat down and fixed his eyes on Tom's face. "Now look. A lot has happened. You need to understand that I did the best I could. I *do* have the situation under control. You have to believe that. It may not be exactly as we planned, but," John paused.

Tom glared at John, trying to absorb what was being said. His breathing began to slow as John continued.

"Now, tell me. What exactly happened here, to the best of your knowledge," John asked.

Daniels took a moment to clear his throat and began. He ended his recollection with, "and that's where I found him dead."

"Yes. Right. Now, I need you to tell me, what did the autopsy report say," John asked.

Tom's face went rigid. He clenched his teeth and spoke in a monotone. "There's never been one."

"What? Did you ask for one?" John asked.

"Of course, you idiot. Sheriff said it must have gotten lost, or some such," Tom answered.

John glanced away and paused before he spoke again. "That could be good. No report, no questions, no nothing," he murmured to himself.

"So that's it? You're not going to tell me anything else?" Tom asked.

"Your sheriff, Dennis Brown came down to see me. Said you and Christina had raised some questions. He was more interested in Porter's state of mind when I saw him last. Nice enough man, but, Tom, you've got to be more careful what you say to him or what he hears from other people. I didn't tell him anything he didn't already know."

"He's not hearing anything from me." Daniels's voice began to increase in volume again. "And I doubt Christina had much to say to him. He's just sticking his nose in. There's not a lot of Sheriffing to do around these parts. Maybe he's bored."

Daniels took a breath and started in again even louder than before. "And John. You're not the one riding the rollercoaster here. You didn't lose your son and you don't have a wife who's losing her mind!"

"Tom, I'm serious here. You have got to keep your temper under control. I don't need to hear your rants and nobody else does either. You're going to make yourself sick. Just be very careful. Now, let's go to the house. I want to spend some time with Jill."

* * *

THE FOLLOWING SATURDAY turned rainy and cool. The pines sagged with the weight of it as if the nurturing moisture had become a burden.

Daniels sat in his office. He reached into the file cabinet for the vodka, his manuscript, clutched in his hand, pleating it as it gave in to the pressure he exerted.

Good enough. It'll do for that group. I'll fix it later.

He checked the time. He might be late getting to the library if he didn't hurry. He grabbed his rain jacket and manuscript and left the shed. The door swung open back and forth with the small bursts of wind letting rain dampen the entryway as he walked from the shed to his Mercedes SUV.

The smell of coffee and lively conversation filled the library's meeting room. Larry opened the meeting and moved on to the readings.

Daniels was first on the list.

He stood, flattened out his papers on the table, and glanced about the room.

"Well," he smiled. "Here we are again."

He cleared his throat.

An uncomfortable silence filled the room while the writers' group waited for Daniels to begin reading.

"Uh. I . . . uh."

The first few sentences were not much changed from his last reading, but his story veered off into new territory soon after the first page of text. Daniels stopped reading his manuscript and began to ramble. People shifted nervously as they heard, "son-of-a-bitch who beat up my boy," and "we planned to kill . . ." but he stopped mid-sentence, blinked hard and picked up his papers. He left the room without explanation.

Larry quickly brought the members attention back to himself and called the next person on his list.

Marianne could barely contain herself a while later when they broke for coffee and treats.

"Mr. LO. What in the world! What have I been telling you about that man? Did anybody check his breath when he came in? For pity's sake. What a disgrace!"

"Now, FP. Hold your tongue there. Obviously he is acting out on some pretty disturbing issues. None of us need to be judging without knowledge of the man's situation." Sheriff Brown's last sentence was said loud enough for everyone in the room to hear.

Murmuring conversation filled the room, heads nodding in agreement, but expressions showing concern and raised eyebrows indicated the writers' minds were still filled with questions.

Brown had his own thoughts. He wondered if Daniels might be losing his mind.

23

Two weeks later John flew up to Tom's and Jill's home again after receiving a tearful call from his sister.

John led Daniels out the front door and upstairs to the office in the shed. Daniels body was stiff with apprehension and his face was set like a plaster mask.

They settled into their chairs as adversaries about to begin verbal battle.

"Tom, you exploded in front of Jill again. Does that help?"

"I don't understand."

"She needs reassurance. You need patience."

"What's that supposed to mean?"

"Self-control."

"You're angry."

"No, frustrated."

"Why are you here?"

"It's time."

"Time?"

"You need to know things."

"What things?"

"Prepare yourself for a shock."

"Prepare myself? *Prepare myself?*"

"He's alive, Tom."

"What? Dittle's alive?" Tom shrieked.

A loud haunting howl from Porter's dog pierced through the room as the two men stared at each other.

"That damned dog of Porter's. A constant reminder." Tom said. "Now, *you* tell me where *you* were that night, and what *you* did," He commanded. "You never bothered to explain to me exactly what you've been doing or what you've done!"

"Wait just a minute Dad," said a voice that came from the shadows in the corner.

Daniels pushed back against his chair for support.

"Christina. Why are you here?"

"To clear things up."

"What could you possibly know?"

Christina looked down and was silent.

"Well, get on with it then, the two of you!" Daniels crossed his arms.

Christina's voice softened and she began.

"Uncle John wasn't here at all that night, Dad. I was."

"You killed Porter?" Daniels asked.

Christina watched her father's face turning red. "Hold on here. Dad, Uncle John is right. You have got to get a hold of yourself. Now listen."

The door to the outside creaked open and they heard the sound of heavy footsteps mounting the stairs. The three turned to see a tall figure appear in the entrance to the room.

Daniels stomped his foot on the floor. John's eyebrows raised high on his forehead, Christina's mouth fell open.

"Brown! What the hell are you doing here?" Daniels asked.

Sheriff Brown kept his attention on them, his expression calm as he dragged a chair close and sat down. His face didn't show emotion or a clue of what ideas were swirling around in his head.

"How long have you been here? You been listening?" Daniels asked.

"Just arrived. I have a theory about your boy's death that I want to share with you. I didn't expect I would find all of you here, but, so much the better. I won't have to repeat it."

"Theory?" John questioned.

"The night Porter died." Brown turned to look directly at Daniels.

"I think all of you were involved in one way or another. There was a plan you and Anderson concocted to get Carson Dittle out of Porter's life for good because of all the trouble he made for him. You planned to kill him and make it look accidental. He would have been given some kind of incentive to go after Porter up here. You'd find him on your property, surprise him, and then shoot him as an intruder. But it all went wrong, didn't it? Somehow Dittle found where Porter was and he killed him, before you could set him up."

The room was so quiet a spider spinning a web could have been heard.

Brown continued. "Daniels, you didn't hear a gunshot probably because of the wind and the lengthy distance from your house to where the murder took place. I think you planned to whisk Porter off somewhere remote so that he could live quietly and recover from Dittle's latest assault on his well-being."

Brown turned his attention to Christina. "I'm not

sure the role you played, Christina, but I think you knew Dittle well enough that you supplied information to your Uncle that would help to convince Dittle to do whatever Dr. Anderson here would have demanded."

Christina's gaze dropped to the floor and she squeezed one side of her mouth into her cheek.

The air in the room became charged but there was no other reaction to his words.

"Now the question is, what did you do with Dittle? According to what I've learned, he's disappeared. Should I be looking for a body?"

Daniels turned to look at Anderson. "Is that what happened?"

No one spoke. A full minute passed.

Brown stood, shook his head back and forth in disbelief, and put his hat back on. His shoulders pressed downward as he exhaled. He was puzzled with Daniels' question to Anderson.

"I can see I'm not going to get anywhere here, today. But I will. Count on it," he said looking at each of them. "Someday, you will realize the right thing to do and I will get the whole story."

The three of them watched as Brown turned away from them and went down the stairs. He closed the outside door with a firm shove.

Brown stood outside the door for a moment. He looked up at the second story of the shed. He stayed close to the door, hoping to overhear their conversation.

Christina sighed aloud. "He was close. But that's not how it went. I found out one day, by accident, what you two were up to. It was wrong. Totally wrong. My dad and my uncle don't just go out and kill someone, for crying out loud! But I knew how to get back at Dittle. You have no idea what I can do and how I could hurt him real bad, and make him do what *I* wanted. And I could keep you two from carrying out your horrible plan."

"Listen, Christina. I don't see where anyone has done anything wrong here. Whatever plans we had didn't work out. Porter's well taken care of, Dittle is out of our hair and no one the wiser. There's no autopsy report and the sheriff can't reopen a case without new evidence."

"But, *we* know Dittle is dead. The Sheriff doesn't know it. Right there is new evidence."

"There's no body to dig up. He's been cremated."

"Bones have DNA. What's going to stop him from getting those?"

"Nobody has them. They were disposed of properly. Scattered. Remember?"

"Oh." She shook her head. John saw tears welling up in her eyes.

"I'm not sure I can live with this," she said.

Daniels looked as if he was confused. "Harrumph. I'm outa here," he said.

"No, you're not, Tom. I came here today to tell you... will you sit down and pay attention? For the life of me I don't know what Jill ever saw in you."

Daniels glared back at his brother-in-law.

"Porter's alive and well taken care of, like we planned. I have to tell you, he does not want to see you or for you to know where he is."

John watched as Daniels eyes moved about the room. "Have you been listening at all?"

"Alive? What about Dittle?" Tom asked.

"He's dead, Dad. That was his body you found."

"What am I to tell Jill?" Daniels asked. His head hung low, his shoulders were rounded.

Quiet enveloped the room like a storm cloud in the distance gathering strength and stalking the landscape for the best place to deposit its growing fury.

"Better to say nothing, in my opinion," John said. "She's going to stay with us permanently, Tom. You are not the caregiver she needs."

Tom stood up and went to John getting close to his face. "You're taking my wife from me?"

"It was her choice."

"Right."

"And that was just brilliant, Tom."

"What."

"Writing about Porter's memoirs."

"So?"

"You stupid, egotistical, uncaring, drunken, self-serving... "

"I'm a damned good writer."

John's eyes opened wide and flew to the ceiling looking for inspiration.

"No, you fool! You keep bringing the subject up to outsiders. Let everyone forget it."

"Forget? That's stupid!"

"Unbelievable!"

Daniels faced his daughter. "Porter's not dead. Doesn't want to see me. My daughter killed Dittle. My wife won't live with me. I'm out of here. I need a drink."

Daniels turned on his heel and moved toward the doorway. He turned back toward Christina and John for a moment. "I *really* need a drink." He headed down the stairs and through the door.

"Dad, nobody killed anybody. If anything, I bullied Dittle into killing himself," Christina said to his back.

Brown heard voices raised in argument and then footsteps coming toward the door where he was still standing. He turned and started toward his car. He was seated and deep in thought as he watched Daniels head for the house.

John walked over to Christina and took her hand in his. "He'll adjust eventually. Christina. And you can't blame yourself for Dittle's death."

"I set him up."

"He set himself up. Your ability to get the evidence and what I knew, we both had enough to put him in prison for a long time, and that is what most likely set him off."

"You could be right," Christina sighed. "Take good care of Porter, please. Tell him I wish him every good thing he can find for his life. And get that darn wolf-dog back to him."

"Oh, and Christina, stay away from that sheriff. He's a smart one."

Christina paused, blinked hard and looked thoughtfully at her uncle.

24

Christina grabbed her coat and hurried down the stairs. She saw that Sheriff Brown was still there, sitting in his car with the engine running. She got to the driver's door, breathless.

Brown pushed the button to open the driver's side window.

"Christina. What is it?"

"We need to talk. Where can I meet you?"

"How about my ranch. If you need privacy, that would be suitable."

"All right. An hour?"

Christina went into the house to say goodbye to her mother. She gave Jill a long emotional hug. "You be happy with Uncle John, Mom. He can help you with anything you need and I'll visit as often as possible."

"Yes. Of course. I'll see you soon then."

Christina didn't bother to look for her father.

The ride out to Brown's ranch gave her time to reflect. She recalled her uncle's words and began to think he may be right; no new evidence could be produced to reopen the case. She felt Sheriff Brown deserved an explanation and confessing her involvement in Dittle's death could release some of the guilt she felt. Dittle had been a beast. The drug use, the horrible things he did to people he chose to harass and the illegal things he participated in were of his own doing. She hadn't intended for him to die. Her idea of retribution was for him to be intimidated and beaten at his own game. Authorities could take care of everything else.

She thought about her father's addiction to alcohol. He needed help, but would he take it if offered? Her mother would be well taken care of until that time. Christina doubted he would ever be capable of caring for her himself. She knew he regarded her Mom as a trophy. Loved her, yes, but still, a trophy. Until he changed he would not be able to see her to the end of her Alzheimer's journey.

Christina felt her cell phone buzzing. She pulled into a side road and answered it.

"It's taken care of," the caller said.

"Thanks. I appreciate that more than you know. I'll be off grid for at least another day. She listened for another moment, and then replied, "Bye."

She visualized the contents of the steel box she had emptied from Dittle's room going up in smoke and the ashes crumbled and dispersed, leaving no evidence.

She bowed her head for a moment, weary. Too much had happened in the last year. Her Granna and Granpa Anderson had both died within hours of each other. They were devoted to each other in life and their deaths so close together seemed right. Uncle John was able to make arrangements, but they both thought it was too much for her mother to absorb only a year after the death of Porter. She often asked her associates to fill in for her wherever necessary during her absence. They had worked together in her grandparents foundation since she was sixteen and she felt confident there would be no breach in security.

Granna and Granpa had prepared her early as a child to become trained to work within a secret arm of the foundation they financed. When Christina reached her sixteenth birthday they had urged her to leave home to begin her tutoring. She acted like a rebellious teenager and used it as a cover for her absence telling them she was off to California to live with a boy friend. Granna had promised to let her mother know that she had kept in touch with her grandparents and was doing well. Christina knew her father would go along with whatever Jill told him.

She loved the responsibility and had immersed herself in computer languages and programs until she became regarded as the best within the foundation. Cybercrimes became her specialty and disguises in dress and voice kept her from discovery. Even her closest associates had been fooled into believing they were dealing with another agent while working on one particularly complicated case.

Christina arrived at Brown's ranch and parked in the driveway near the front porch. She drew a long breath and climbed the five stairs that led to the front door.

Her soft rap on the door produced the sheriff immediately. He ushered her in, taking her coat to hang up, and showed her the way to his kitchen.

"I have fresh coffee, if you like."

"Thanks. That would be great. Black, please."

"Coming right up."

He placed their filled mugs on the table. He thought

she wore concern on her face like a mother tending her child's scraped knee.

"What is it you wish to talk about, Christina?"

"I think you deserve to know the truth. What you do with it is your call."

Both took a sip from their mug.

"There's a lot to tell you. To begin with, Porter wasn't the only one harassed by Carson Dittle. He started on me in high school and continued while I was away. He learned how to hack into computers. That's when I decided I needed to learn that skill as well. It led to a high-paying job, and I was better at it than Dittle. In his computer I found unbelievable stuff. Threats to my brother I know he carried out, and some to girls on the campus where Porter went to college. I got in touch with Uncle John because I was sure Dittle's actions were affecting the success of Porter's treatments. I also hacked into Uncle John's computer. I was able to get into his office and desk files when I made a visit there. You don't need to know how and you never heard me say it. Anyway, I found notes between Dad and Uncle John outlining how they would get rid of Dittle. I wasn't going to let that happen. Besides, I was sure I could get to Dittle in my own way and put a stop to everything. I talked to Uncle John and told him some of what I would be able to do. He agreed not to carry out the first part of their plan. And you were right. They wanted to lure him up to Dad's place and shoot him for trespassing. They were going to plant something on him that they would claim he stole.

"I decided to contact Dittle and arrange a meeting. Told him how much I hated Porter and wanted to get rid of him."

Brown listened as she detailed her activities. He got up and poured more coffee.

She continued, uninterrupted. "Dittle ate it up. I had plenty of evidence about his computer activities to use against him if he resisted, but I never had to. I had copies of files he stole from Uncle John and evidence of the girls he bullied and attacked. He followed me like a puppy dog. We drove up to Mom and Dad's together. He tried to overpower me at one point on the way and had become somewhat unstable by the time we arrived. That scared me a little. I conned him into a little play-acting. He followed my instructions and played the part of Porter and since he provided the gun I had told him Porter would use to kill himself, he began to demonstrate how it would be used. I did make sure the gun was not loaded; I want to be clear about that. I checked it out thoroughly. Then I handed it to him. Dittle held the gun, kind of fiddled around with it, and then put it into his mouth. I got really nervous then; he acted so weird. I begged him to quit fooling around. Geez. He was such an ass! He pulled out the clip and showed me it was empty. But as soon as he did it and put it back on, he pulled the trigger."

Quiet engulfed the room as Brown listened in silence.

"Obviously, Dittle didn't know guns like I do. After he went down, I took a closer look. I realized that particular gun carries a bullet in the chamber separate from the clip. He couldn't have known it was there, much less how to remove it. So you see, it was an accident. I got out of there and..."

Christina put her elbow on the table and leaned her mouth and chin in her hand before she resumed speaking. "Dittle was broken. You only had to look at him and you knew he felt useless and powerless. Even then he continued to act out how Porter would kill himself. He unwittingly took his own life instead."

Neither spoke for a moment until Brown got up from his chair, pushing it aside with his foot. "Dittle is dead. So where in the world was Porter while all that was going on?" he asked.

"I asked him to meet me at the far side of the woods at a specified time. I knew he would show because I told him that I had figured out a way to get Dittle out of his life forever. The second part of Uncle John and Dad's plan was to whisk Porter away to a remote location where he could live quietly and recover, away from family and stress. Uncle John was prepared to fly Porter out of there immediately. We couldn't let Dad in on those plans because Porter wouldn't cooperate unless we assured him that Dad knew nothing. I left without Mom or Dad even knowing I'd ever been there."

"What happened to the gun?"

"I couldn't leave that kind of evidence there, so I grabbed it just before Dad came outside. I took it to people who know how to make it disintegrate. Completely."

"How do you know people like that? What do they do? Melt it down?"

"Those details aren't important. I know people because my computer takes me to world's you've likely never heard of."

"I may decide to confiscate your computer."

"Not possible. I destroyed it and my cell phone before I made any contacts with Dittle."

"You are thorough. But how did you keep up communications with Dittle and your brother if you destroyed your cell phone?"

"I can't leave any evidence that might interfere with my brother staying healthy. I have disposable phones, shall we say."

"Do you know where Porter is?"

"Yes."

"Your uncle?"

"Yes. But Porter informed him he would ditch the place if we ever disclosed his whereabouts."

"What was your purpose in telling me this? You could have left it alone."

"I was sure you were not about to let it go. You said as much when you left today. And I needed to get it off my chest. I feel guilty about leading Dittle to his own death."

"The gun could have cleared you. The chamber that held the fatal bullet."

"Bullet discharged from there? How could anyone prove for certain it came from that hidden chamber?"

"Do you ever miss any detail?"

"It's not an option."

"You might want to think about changing careers. I bet there is a police academy somewhere waiting for a person with your investigative detail."

"So, is this the end of it?" she asked.

"I'm sure there is more to be played out than either of us is aware of."

"Then, I'll be going."

"I don't have to tell you to take care of yourself, because I know you will."

For the first time that day, Christina smiled. She put on her coat, thanked Brown for the coffee and left.

Brown scratched his head. What she didn't know was

that Sheriff Brown had checked back with the police in Tucson. They didn't have the DNA samples from Dittle. They had sent it to a lab. He had checked with the lab and they confirmed the date received, but informed him that a small explosion in the lab had messed up any samples waiting for analysis. Even if they had found it and the autopsy report turned up, the DNA from the body would only confirm that the DNA wasn't from Porter's body, and they would have had nothing to compare it to.

Of course, none of that matters now. I know now, some of what Christina told me isn't entirely true. With all that special training she is still a youngster with a lot to learn. She should have wondered why I let her go.

* * *

A KNOCK ON HIS front door a day earlier had startled Sheriff Brown from an afternoon snooze.

Two men stood on the front porch. Brown was sure they were government men. They were dressed in dark suits and ties, and wore dark glasses. He invited them in but they refused his offer to join him in the living room.

"We're here on confidential business."

"I see. What do I have to do with it?"

"Your inquiries into the background of Carson Dittle must cease. And any interrogation or investigation of any sort about Christina Daniels cannot be allowed."

"I am not sure why I should comply."

"Simply put, Ms Daniels is contracted by a privately-funded foundation. Her work is vital to citizen's security on many important fronts. To protect the information she provides, the government works in concert with the foundation to provide privacy at every level. She will not be informed of our visit to you, and it is expected you will not give her any indication we have been in contact with you."

"What kind of foundation is it you refer to, and who funds it?"

"That is public information. The nature of their work is not."

"My guess is it is the Anderson's. My background checks showed they were a wealthy family in Phoenix and funded several worthwhile causes. What Christina is involved in must be part of one of them."

"The family had the foresight to realize what the internet could bring about. They've taken the necessary steps to insure the stabilization of the economy and to protect the security of citizen's personal information. For that we are grateful. I'm sure you can understand the implications."

"There will always be persons who will risk everything to unravel it."

"More reason to protect those who seek to find the perpetrators."

"Of course. I understand. Gentlemen?"

Brown directed them back to his front door. He closed it behind them with a firm, slow hand. His head nodded up and down as the puzzle pieces fell together. *Some things just go away because they can. As well as some people.*

25

Sheriff Brown contemplated the circumstances he saw as bizarre. *I've nowhere to go with this information. There's nothing to be gained and nothing I could possibly dig up to re-open Porter's supposed death. That kid, Dittle. The world is probably better off without him. But who knows if somehow he could have been counseled and brought around to lead a productive and useful life? No one will ever know how he died. I learned that both his parents were, in fact, deceased and he had no siblings. Relatives of the family were non-existent as far as any records I dug up.*

He reached for the phone and dialed Marianne's number. He let it ring once and then hung it up. *I can't tell her anything anyway. I'll just have to let this one go. I think I'd feel better if I could find out how Porter is doing. There has to be a positive side to this somewhere.*

* * *

The mountains of Northern Idaho seemed to protrude forever up into the cloudless summer skies. Porter Daniels walked the familiar trail in the early morning cool until he reached the lake as he had done many times. He perched on a low-lying ledge while enjoying the view. Meditating for several minutes calmed his mind. He reached into his backpack and unwrapped the energy bar he had brought and bit into it. He took a swig from his insulated water bottle, unscrewed the attached cup and filled it with water for his dog. His new life opened up possibilities he'd never imagined and he was actually doing something to help others as well as himself. He couldn't think of a better way to spend his days.

Uncle John had arranged for him to be enrolled in an experimental program to help find newer and better treatments for bipolar disorder, the umbrella for many mental illnesses known to afflict so many. The new facility was built in a style to minimize its intrusion on the wilderness. Set far back into the forest and high above the valley below, the windowed structure provided views to Montana and Washington.

As part of an innovative and forward thinking study he had volunteered for a method called transcranial direct current stimulation, a non-invasive technique using a very weak direct electrical current that is passed through the cerebral cortex and he and his medical team felt it had helped.

Christina sent mail to a post office box and Porter wrote her back regularly. He took out the latest letter from his sister and reread it. She and his Uncle John had remained his only contact with his former life. It helped to ease the guilt he felt for never contacting their mother. In her letter, Christina assured him Mom was doing well, even better than expected. Dad had completed a year-long in-residence dual counseling program for alcohol dependence and life-changing events. Christina thought he may be able to reunite with Mom in Tucson in a home specializing in Alzheimer patient care.

Porter's accommodations were located in the east wing of the large building whose foundation had been created from the many rocks available in the area. The sign above the doorway indicated the donor's names and reads ANDERSON HALL. The brass plaque attached to the wall was engraved with the words: "In memory of Granna and Granpa Anderson, benefactors to those in need."

The hope was that the experimental procedures and medications would one day help people with Alzheimer's and also those with Parkinson's disease.

His aging companion, the half-wolf-half-dog, Lala-sa, was always at his side and no longer howled for his company.

THE END